MW00608566

If All Would Be Utopia

Raina Nascimento

Dedicated to my children. I promise to always be a source of unconditional love for you.

This is a work of fiction. Names, characters, places, and incidents
either are the product of the author's imagination or are used
fictitiously. Any resemblance to actual persons, living or dead,
events, or locales is entirely coincidental.
Copyright © 2020 by Raina M. Nascimento
All rights reserved. No part of this book may be reproduced or
used in any manner without written permission of the copyright
owner except for the use of quotations in a book review.
First edition September 2020
Book design by Raina M. Nascimento
ISBN 978-1-7356068-1-1 (paperback)

CONTENTS

CONTENTS CONTINUED

PROLOGUE

SANDRA

I had a dream last night and, in it, I died. I lounged upon the clouds with angels of light, eating chocolates, and laughing. Oh, how I yearn for that freedom. Will only death bring it to me? Sometimes after he goes to work, I sit and ponder if I am already dead. If, at one time, I was alive and was *so wretched* that I went to hell. Surely, this is what it is like. But then, why do I grow older? Being stuck somewhere for eternity would halt the aging process, of this I am certain.

This morning, much to my dismay, I am awake. I am one day older, one day closer to death and, I pray, freedom from this living hell.

TIFFANY

I had the worst dream last night (or was it this morning?) I don't know, and it doesn't matter anyway. Whatever. There was this guy – a super sexy guy – calling me names, and then he hit me really hard in the chest. After that, I just woke up. I wish I could remember exactly what he looked like. I know he was FINE. He definitely had dark hair because I remember the beautiful contrast of his tan skin next to my blonde hair. That's about it, so I guess I don't really remember much at all.

Time to get up. Ugh. I usually love going to work, but I'm not feeling that shit today. I'm so sick of my boss hitting on me. *On us, really.* He's short and bald and fat and ugly and – well, you get the picture. Gross! This man thinks he's AMAAAAZING because he owns an itty-bitty company tucked way back in the corner of the fucking ghetto. *eye roll* A & A Chemicals has got to be his one legacy because I don't see any other shit in his life that he has going for him. There's not a winning personality there, I'll tell you that. He's going on divorce number two, and he sells detergents and soaps for a living. Trust me, it's really nothing extravagant or impressive. Now, don't get me wrong, I came up being taught (and wholeheartedly believe) that *any* kind of honest work is admirable. I don't care what you do to take care of you and yours, believe that. Work is work, and if you work hard, you're good in my book.

But boss man is just another pervert, and they're a dime a dozen. The other day he asked Claire (from customer service) and I if we ever "run out" of spit. We were putting together 300-page binders of MSDS sheets for all of the chemicals we carry. We need these for all clients, prospective clients, businesses, etc. It's important for the environment that our clients know how to properly use and dispose of these products correctly. Also, who wants Uncle Sam raping their bank accounts for non-compliance when it's incredibly simple to just follow the rules and put together binders? It is important that we get these finished. Instead, we end up entertaining disgusting convos with whack-ass, real-life Homer Simpson over here.

"Hey ladies," Bob drawled, slithering into the room. He smiled, but don't get it twisted. It wasn't cute or inviting in any way whatsoever. It was clear from the get-go his intentions were anything but kind. He looked sinister and hungry. His bloodshot eyes narrowed as he asked, "Tell me, do you gals ever run out of spit?"

"Ew," Claire said out loud. She glanced at me, sighed, and rolled her eyes. We knew what was coming.

I answered him dryly, "We have three sets of glands in and around our mouths that continually produce saliva, so it's not super accurate to say we can 'run out' of spit, *BOSS*," I like to emphasize the word "boss" right before he's gonna drop a nasty, perverted line to his subordinates. This little-minded man is so damn predictable. It's just a little test. Will Bob locate his moral compass today? Nope, not even once. Not ever.

"Mmmm," he moaned a little. It's a disturbing sound that makes my stomach turn. "Well, after you're finished, I could put some of it to better use. Just saying, ladies. What a waste of that endless glandular production."

I glared at him, "We use fingertip moisteners. You should probably speak with Paul in Purchasing if you're concerned with your work negatively impacting your salivary production. He can order those for you. Or maybe you should consider seeking professional help if you feel your salivary production is under par. We all care about your well-being." I smiled at him sweetly, my voice dripping with obvious sarcasm.

Claire's chin looked like it would hit the floor, her jaw dropped so fast. We gotta work on that girl's poker face, I thought to myself. But Bob just laughed a little to himself and walked out. Of course, he couldn't resist tossing a little wink in our direction before slinking out the door. Does he think I won't quit or sue him? I can get another receptionist position somewhere else. It's really not that hard. (That's what she said.) But, seriously, he's such a dirty old man: He's 48 and I'm barely 23. GROSS!

I suppose it is time to prepare for another day of work. I always feel so much better after I shower. He's never here when I get out, so sometimes I pretend that I'm single again. A fresh start. I prepare some breakfast and imagine a strapping young man is lying in my bed. I took him home from Caesar's Bar last night, and he was hungry for more than just food. Yes, a one-night stand. That is exactly what I would love.

Want to know the best part about a one-night stand? They leave.

And

Never

Come

Back.

Not like *him*. He is always messing about in my business causing grief, pain, and alienation. Oh, bother. Now I've gone and spilled my coffee.

When I am on break at work, I lose myself in a countless number of books. Any book will do, it would seem. Whether engrossed by one page or one thousand, every story is my sanctuary. When I'm stocking the shelves of Binded Books – my little taste of part-time self-sufficiency – I read the back of every single true crime story, always wondering if it will be my fate to grace the covers of these mass media paperbacks. Will my tales of woe someday grip these same readers standing next to me? Lord, if I make it through this treacherous life I've created, I'd gladly write the book myself. But published? No, I'd think not. I'll leave that to the professionals. The driven. The powerful. You know the type. Ladies with graceful, long strides that bustle from here to there in pencil skirts over perfect bods, complete with stiletto heels. That's not my style. Of course, on occasion, I've imagined being published. It's not like I've *never* had a dream before, but it's not crossed my mind in years. Until recently, that is, when it suddenly resurfaced out of nowhere.

Typically, my heart is where dreams go to die.

Oh, my heavens! When I think back, it all seems so childish. I used to be certain that it was my destiny – a muse calling me – to create. To mold this English verse, bend language to my whim, and manipulate and entrance audiences. At one time, the words effortlessly flowed from my beautiful and mighty pen, and I'd imagine my work tugging at the heartstrings of millions. It was my first love, long before I met him. His coarse words and sharp tongue steered me away from my true love and, somewhere along the line, I lost interest in pursuing any kind of writing career at all. If I am being honest, it would be more appropriate to say I lost interest in everything. The transition was so subtle, I suppose it went unnoticed.

And now, a decade and a half later, here I am. Every book I shelf – every fiction, fantasy, and even horror – I wonder if it could have been mine. Where is this renewed sense of wonder inside of me stemming from? I'll not question it. Instead, I'll enjoy my unexpected reprise from reality and expect these imaginary longings to be short-lived.

CHAPTER 1

Another day is almost over, and I still have no idea what I want to be "when I grow up." I've been going to Bauer Community College off and on since I graduated from high school six years ago, but it seems like nothing is right for me. Sometimes I withdraw from my classes because I don't like my teachers or, once, because my sociology teacher had an accent so strong, I couldn't even understand where he said he was from. Why even bother, do you feel me?

Right now I'm sitting at Caesar's Bar. I've never been here before, but it seems super chill. Plush, blood-red carpet and black leather bar stools with comfortable backs. That shit is important! I can't be falling off the back of a stool. Ohhh, but that carpet is not a shabby landing. I slip off a stiletto to run my toes through it, and I'm feeling like I need new goals in my life that include this level of fanciness.

They have the most amazing paintings I have ever seen in my life upon these walls. Well, that's not saying much. I don't spend a whole lot of time at the art gallery, you know? Actually, I've never been to one at all. One time in high school, we had a field trip to the art museum, but I skipped school that day. High school priorities AKA boyyys. The only pictures I ever see are the ones taken with a digital camera or, mostly, just cell phone pics. Cells have some bomb features, though. Can you even tell the difference between that and a professional camera? I wonder, but not enough to educate myself on the matter. I asked the bartender (who introduced himself as Tom) if he knew what this kind of painting is called. They all kinda look similar but kinda different at the same time. There are ones with red, white, and black splotches with lines throughout. In another, it looks like the paint is dripping down the silver background, but it's obviously a finished work. It's just like that on purpose. He said they're called abstract paintings, and the artist is someone named Hunyar. That's the last name.

I left my vodka martini sitting on the bar to get a closer look. "A. Hunyar" was scribbled in red paint in the lower right-hand corner. I could feel Tom's deep blue eyes burning into my back as I studied this newfound discovery.

I turned to look at him. "This does something for me," I said.

"Me, too," he replied. "It gets on my nerves."

I love the coffee shop at Binded. It's so quaint and intimate. The aroma of espresso lingers in the air, tickling and teasing the nostrils of hundreds of patrons daily. People sit around chatting in all available spaces, relaxing in the plump reclining chairs, curled together on the couches of polyester, gathered around tables in the café, or just randomly sitting around on the floor. I take a deep and satisfying inhalation of breath. This is my life. *I am actually alive here.*

Not like at home when I'm with him. Venomous words and an unkind touch from the man who vowed to take care of me until death, do us part. The only thing he takes care of is making sure *I do die* someday, not that it was an uncertain aspect of life in the first place. The only reason I'm not already gone is because of this journal. Writing down events and feelings has certainly saved my sanity on more than one occasion throughout these painful years.

My mother always taught me to write everything down. "Life's best and worst must be recorded. Only after reading and rereading can one understand. With understanding comes knowledge and, with that, wisdom. Only with wisdom can you achieve *anything*. The others are merely stepping stones to build character in order to reach your true destiny."

At 32-years-old, I question if I have achieved any amount of wisdom at all. There are still a lot of things that I have yet to understand. One thing I do know is not a day has gone by that I haven't recorded life's best and worst between these covers. The best has been, in recent years, days spent at Binded. The worst has always been my husband: *him*.

I'm at the art museum right now sitting in front of a painting by a man named Pablo Picasso. I walked all through this place and, don't get me wrong, I loved all of it. But his stuff – well, to me – is the best! I always pass this place on my way to A & A Chemicals, but I never even knew I liked art, so I never came in to see what it was about. I had no idea what I was missing out on. How could I live for 23 years and just now realize this? So I'm looking at Mr. Picasso's painting of a lady, but she doesn't really look *normal*. Everything is all spazzed out. Like, her eyes aren't the right size, and you kind of have to guess if she's sitting at a table or... something else? I'm curious and starting to wonder now. I know it seems like a stupid idea, but I wonder if I could be good at painting. I mean, nothing has ever made me feel this way before, so if it is stirring up this much passion inside of me, I can't be horrible, right? Sure, why not? I'm going to the art store, and then I'll give it a go. Whatevs. I have nothing to lose anyway. I feel so lost and undecided about life.

I remember it like it was yesterday: my day of bliss. It's the day every little girl dreams of. Okay. Maybe not *every* girl, but I certainly did. Ahhhh, my wedding was such a lovely social event. I have read my tattered diary pages over and over, wondering where it all went wrong for us. I was so young – fresh out of high school – when I married Anthony. Not quite 18, and all I could think about was how much I thought I was in love. *I was in love.* I cannot minimize it or pretend I didn't have real feelings for this monster. He was such a different man in those days. That was my impression of him, at least. I know now it was merely the impression he wanted to make sure I believed.

I graduated at the top of my class and was planning to attend a prestigious university in the fall. One does not need to be uneducated or of low intelligence to end up in my position. When he asked me to marry him, I didn't give it a second thought. Choosing between a career or a family with the man of my dreams didn't seem like any kind of decision at all. The date was set, and we were wed two months later at my parents' lavish estate. I spent half of August and my 18th birthday on a cruise ship in Europe. It seemed like heaven at the time. Of course, Anthony still had to keep current with his workload, so most days I didn't even see him until well past sunset. In those moments, lounging on the deck in the evenings while sipping expensive champagne and watching the beautiful sunset over the water, next to such a handsome and charismatic man, I had so many dreams.

First on the agenda? A family! He will be such a good father, I thought to myself as he lovingly draped his jacket over my shoulders at the first sign of a shiver. He kissed me on the forehead so tenderly, and I smiled up at his twinkling gaze. I still pray I never forget the way he looked at me on those first magical nights after we wed. Sometimes I forget what he looked like when there was love in his gaze. Even if it was all an act, I still want to remember him that way. I wanted children and dinner promptly at five o'clock. PTA meetings, movie nights at home, and vacations with extended family or friends to get away from all the hustle and bustle of life. We never had children, and I am so grateful for that fact. My so-called Prince Charming lost that sparkle in his eyes not long after those romantic nights on the deck. *At least for me, he did.*

I have everything I need to begin exploring my artistic side, but I did take some shortcuts because I don't make that much money. The perv only pays me $12 an hour. I got all of the regular colors of acrylic paints: all of the colors of the rainbow and a bigger one each of black and white. I didn't get brown because I don't really like it, so I think it would be a waste of money because it probably won't get used. The lady at Mae's Art Supplies was trying to talk me into an easel and a pallet. For real, she tried to sell me loads of shit I don't need.

Finally, I said, "I appreciate all of your help, but I don't even know if I can paint yet." I shrugged and she walked away. I ended up with a roll of double-sided tape, a book of canvas paper, two brushes, and something called "gloss." According to my online search, it's supposed to make the picture smooth and shiny, but I didn't get the brand I saw online so who knows how comparable it will be. I've taped the canvas paper to my wall (easel problem solved), and I've got all of my paints on a big serving dish that my mom got me for Christmas one year (pallet problem solved).

Now there's just one "minor" detail to take care of: I DON'T KNOW WHAT THE FUCK I'M DOING! Do I draw a design first? If I *do* draw it first, should it be on a separate piece of paper or directly onto the canvas paper? Do I mix this gloss stuff into my paint or put it directly on the canvas? If I put it on the canvas, does it go on before or after I paint? Great, I'm completely overwhelmed and lost. I need a book or I'll risk falling into a massive rabbit hole searching online for all of this. I guess I'll go to Binded Books. They have everything there.

Okay. I just got back from Binded (after being in there for an eon) and it's no wonder artists are starving! Art instruction books are mega-expensive, no joke. I was looking at a couple of different ones trying to decide which one to get, and then I saw the prices and almost fainted. One was ninety-five bucks. Seriously, fuck that!

I went to the information counter at the front of the store and talked to a lady named Sandra. She was super nice. She helped me find four instruction books each in my price range of $20 or less, and I'm pretty sure she knew the entire store inside and out. She never even looked anything up on the computer. Sandra just heard what I wanted, waved her hand, and instructed me to follow her. She has such a pleasant voice, too. We talked for about half an hour, and she gave me so much encouragement.

"Paint through your heart," she advised me. "The beauty of your art is already in your soul. Hands are merely an instrument for you to convey your message to others. If a professional paints without passion, his will collect dust. If an amateur conducts his soul onto canvas by way of his hands, he will collect respect. And all competent artists sell tremendously after death, so there's always that route!" She winked playfully, and I was so intrigued by her aura.

I was ridiculously nervous to start something like this, but I'm feeling way better after talking with Sandra. *I just wish she was happy.* I mean, she didn't *say* anything specific that made me think that, but there was something really heavy I saw deep in her eyes whenever she spoke. Even when she gave me that little wink at the end of our convo, her eyes seemed distant somehow. Detached. What was it about her that I sensed? Ahhhh, I know. It was despair.

There are certain times in life that one should evaluate difficult situations before reacting. The ideal person bites their tongue, always taking careful inventory of possible consequences, as opposed to impulsively leaping into action. Perhaps a cleansing inhalation could be afforded while quickly pondering different outcomes. The majority of the time, I am this level-headed and sensible person I speak of. Typically, I don't need to utilize that cleansing breath because I am predictably compliant. I am steady, constant, and dependable. Patient to a fault, some may say. But even the most passive woman can be pushed beyond her breaking point.

It could happen to anyone, right? A mother, when someone is a threat to her child; a driver, during a long commute after reaching for a cigarette finding none; or a wife, who has been irreparably emotionally damaged for many,

many,

long,

dreadful

years.

Ask me where my defiance has gotten me today. What have I gone and done, now that I've lost my temper? I retaliated, and it only served to make matters worse for my own existence. Like an impulsive child, all logic and sensibility vanished in one instant, and I was completely ruled by my heart instead of my head. After all these years, I had finally snapped. Unfortunately, I was less than prepared for this hot-headed sort of life, so I did the only thing my instincts told me to do.

Run, you fool!

CHAPTER 2

I have so many ideas about the possibilities of creating different art pieces, but I'm still so nervous. I am going to begin by painting with my eyes closed. I know it sounds crazy, but this is the way I will feel more comfortable starting. If I'm painting from my soul as Sandra told me to do, then why do I *need* to look at the paper? If I'm "conducting through my hands" then I should be able to *feel* what it looks like before I actually see it, right? I'll still look when choosing colors. I'm not trying to do it without ANY direction.

Oh Em Gee… Maybe I AM crazy. Then again, maybe crazy will help. I don't know much about Pablo Picasso, but I read that he said he could draw "like Raphael" when he was young. "But it has taken me my whole life to learn to draw like a child," he added. Sanity is obviously overrated. Now, back to that blindfold.

Let me start at the beginning. Last night, I made dinner for Anthony. It was a splendid meal, and I slaved over the hot stove for hours to prepare it. A beautiful dinner that ended in pure disaster. I would love to have a peaceful day with Anthony – the kind of day that allows my mind to wander back to better days and allows my heart to live in denial. I'm not asking for dysfunctional, long-term denial. Just one day of bliss, where all of the sorrows of this life are forgotten. To forget for even a moment sounds incredibly satisfying.

He must've had a rough day at the office. The mere sight of the table was obviously underwhelming to him. On the menu were artichokes stuffed with ricotta and prosciutto, lamb flavored with lemon juice and parsley, and pasta con broccoli.

"What's all this?" he demanded, taking a long swig of Chardonnay straight from the bottle. *A bad sign.* The candlelight reflected in his dark and angry, blank eyes – the windows to his soul, as the saying goes. I tried to be audible when I told him it would be enjoyable to sit down together and have a nice meal.

"I thought it would please you," I answered meekly. He demanded to know what I had done. He accused me of having a guilty conscience. I kept repeating myself. "I just wanted to sit down together. I thought a pleasant meal would be nice. I'm so sorry," I whispered, staring down at my hands folded obediently in my lap.

Louder and louder, he reprimanded me for things I have never even *thought* to do like sleep with another man. Sure, just the other day I romanticized the idea, but not about an actual person. It's not like the thought was rooted in reality in any way whatsoever. I don't even keep the company of a man. I've no male friends at all. Or *anyone*, for that matter.

I shall reflect on why I was being reprimanded, lest I should forget and make the same awful mistake that sent my husband into a rampage. It was because I made a lovely dinner. And what if I had not made dinner? No, no, that would have been wrong as well. Do you see it? There is no way to win; he will always remain unsatisfied.

His irrational anger will never cease.

He was yelling at such a volume that I continuously flinched every few seconds. It was so dreadfully loud, I retreated to a place deep inside my head. I cannot even comprehend screaming at that volume. It felt as if he was getting larger with every accusation, filling up the entirety of the space around me. Everything was vibrating as it echoed and boomed, bouncing off of the walls around us. I felt so small.

"Who are you screwing, you disgusting bitch? Look at me when I speak to you, fat whore! What have you done behind my back? You're nothing, do you hear me? You are literally nothing without me. No one would *ever* want you." I'm not sure what else was said. I just *poof* wasn't there anymore. Checked out, not present, gone. It's beautifully ironic, isn't it? *Almost as if I really am no one. Nonexistent.*

Briefly and in slow motion, I witnessed a scene I no longer felt I was actually a party to. From the corner of the room where I cowered, after stumbling hastily from the table, I saw the dish holding the lemon-juice-covered lamb chops – a small portion of the dinner that took three hours to prepare from scratch – fiercely crash to the floor. The dish shattered, spitting bits of white china all around my feet and, as the blood spilled from my toes onto the floor, my head felt as if someone had taken an ax to it.

Suddenly, to even my own surprise, I became a brewing volcanic monster, spewing hatred in his direction. A fire rushed down my spine that has never been felt by my body before, and my face flushed with an intense heat I am unaccustomed to. No, I have never experienced anger of this magnitude. It coursed through my veins, my newfound high making me quick and, in an instant, my husband was covered in scorching hot (and delicious) homemade pasta con broccoli. I had eaten a small portion before he arrived home. At least my famous noodles were reveled by one of us before meeting their untimely demise. Before he could register what had happened, I was locked away in the bedroom with my prize: my beloved artichokes. Had they not survived the conflict, I could very well be facing a lengthy prison sentence at this very moment.

I don't mean that last bit. I'm not too sure where that came from. Highly out of character. Anger got the best of me, and now I cannot bear the thought of how I will be punished for this unacceptable deed. I haven't seen Anthony since the incident a few hours ago, and I couldn't be more thankful he didn't break down our heavy bedroom door. He likely went out with his best friend,

Jack Daniels.

I did it, and I'm amazing! Not that it was ever in question that I am totally awesome, but just saying. I'm a painter! Well, not a professional... YET. Okay, okay. I only did it for the first time, but it made my heart feel so *whole*. How could I not feel like I am walking on sunshine right now? I did just what Sandra said to do, and I painted the most wonderful things! First different colored trees. NO BROWN. LOL. Then I painted a beautiful sky with big, puffy white clouds and a rainbow. And just like Forrest Gump when he kept running and running *and running*, I kept painting and painting until there was not a single canvas paper left to be used. There are 16 pieces in all, including the one I got mad at and ripped up, but I felt so much regret afterward that I taped it back together. Artists are passionate, so whatevs. I put it back together out of order, though, and it's actually my favorite piece! I know that I just met Sandra, but I wonder if it would be weird to show up to Binded with a coffee for her. And a few of my paintings to show her, of course. She seems so personable, I'm sure she would welcome the company. Right now, though, I am going to grab a drink at Caesar's. I absolutely have to tell Tom that I made some art that was totally inspired by A. Hunyar. It will annoy him, for sure. I'm lowkey looking forward to seeing him. Maybe I have a little crush on him. I love his company, and I hope he will appreciate my company all the same. Maybe it will be slow tonight so we can get in some extra conversation.

I stayed barricaded in our bedroom for several hours. At first, I just sat there heaving and shaking uncontrollably. Surely, this must be comparable to a seizure. Panic was in full control of my body. Every sound echoed loudly in my ears, and I thought he was coming after even the slightest creak. But I realized eventually that he was, indeed, no longer home. I was alone, praise God. He likely welcomed the chance to run to – I guess I don't really know – wherever he goes. I began eating the only surviving portion of our beautiful meal which, even under such horrible circumstances, tasted absolutely divine. Martha Stewart would have been proud because the leaves of the artichoke were steamed and seasoned to absolute perfection. I had gone back and forth between a dipping sauce on the side or incorporating the sauce into my seasoning, and I am so happy I settled on the latter. Had I gone the other route, I'd be eating some bland artichoke leaves because I know a sauce either wouldn't have lasted through the havoc or would've been overlooked in my hasty retreat from the dining room.

This is the highlight of my day, I suppose. Sprawled out on a bare marble floor and alone. Locked away in the bedroom but, for once, a deeply satisfying look painted across my face. Rarely does the bedroom hold such a treat for me! Not only did the food leave me feeling better, but my tear-stained cheek and battered body welcomed what the cold, hard floor offered for my injuries. My thoughts went again and again to Anthony's face the moment he realized I was – *dare I say* – standing up for myself. I nibbled somewhat contently and couldn't help but chuckle a little at this long-awaited turn of events. After my artichoke feast, I crept out of my hideaway and peered cautiously around every corner of the house to be absolutely positive my husband had left.

He certainly was gone at that time, and he's not returned since. That was several days ago now, and perhaps I have finally met my demise when he decides to make an appearance again. If I am really fortunate, it will lead to my divorce instead of death. I'll never be brave enough to file myself. Good riddance that he hasn't yet returned, as far as I am concerned. These have, sadly, been the happiest two consecutive days I've had over the past decade. Maybe I should be a pinch nervous about where he is. Could he be lying in a gutter, bloated from death, and reeking of his own feces? Doubtful. He is probably holed up in a sleazy motel with some cheap hooker. Not really. It would be a nice hotel. But, alas, I know this quiet life has to end sometime. I'll not find peace after my tantrum, of this I am sure.

"Tom Tom, bo bom, banana fanna fo fom, me my mo mom... Tom!" I sang before I had even gone all the way through the mirrored doors of Caesar's Bar. I was so damn embarrassed after I saw he was deep in conversation with a gentleman at the end of the bar. I plopped down in a seat at the other side so it wouldn't seem like I was eavesdropping.

Surprisingly, Tom looked up and said, "Tiff! Come on over here. We were just talking about you."

"Me?" I questioned as if there would be another "Tiff" in the empty bar. I felt my cheeks start to burn and walked over to join them.

"This guy here is really into that artsy-fartsy crap that you like." The man smiled and his brown eyes got all squinty. I absolutely adore that quality, when someone smiles with their entire face instead of just their mouth. He was very handsome. The kind of man who would sip champagne in front of a fire on a rug covered in rose petals, offering caviar as an appetizer to the professional-like meal he prepared. *That* kind of handsome. But, hey, it's just a guess.

"I was just telling Tom that I follow Hunyar's work very

closely, and he started ranting about a crazy customer who loves that one," he pointed to the abstract that I had previously admired. "The thought had crossed my mind that Tom could be the crazy one. Of course, it's been confirmed now that I have met you. Hi there, beautiful, everyone here calls me –"

"Tee," Tom finished for him. "And it's not because that is what he drinks unless it's a Long Island."

"Tom, you know I'm a whiskey and soda man. Although, I do enjoy a nice glass of wine from time to time. Wouldn't you agree, um... I apologize, I didn't catch your name."

"She didn't throw it," Tom smirked proudly, like the smart ass he obviously is.

"Tiffany. My name is Tiffany."

"Well, Tiffany, it is such a pleasure to make your acquaintance. What kind of wine do you like?"

"Chablis blanc," I answered, studying his chiseled features.

"Tom. One bottle of Chablis, please."

"Oh no," I stammered. "I couldn't."

"Nonsense," he corrected me. "We're going to celebrate. Your finest bottle, my good man!"

"Celebrate? What could we possibly celebrate together?

We just met."

"That, beautiful stranger, *is* our celebration," he answered smoothly. It wasn't like a creepy, short, fat, bald, perverted owner of a chemical company kind of answer, though. This was the sly, flirty "I'm gonna wine and dine you" kind. I was right about this man. His look fits the part.

I positively dread my husband's return. Should I pray to God that he leaves me as a widow to feign my grief? What would I grieve, exactly? The loss of another day of torture, the prevention of a predator's attack, or the risk of disease, whether sexually transmitted or stress-induced? The blame of my misery lies with him, but I know it is my cross to bear. And what of my misery? Shall it die with him, or have I become a miserable person myself? After so many years, I know not. My husband hits me, yes, but does all of the blame belong with him? Do I not lie next to him by choice? Do I not walk under his hand to be scolded like a child? By sleeping under the same shingled roof, I take this blame alongside him. By staying, I am condemning myself to this fate.

If ever I left, what would I even gain? I assure you, my name has never been on the deed to this house. A house of shame and nothing more, why would I even want it? I hold no skills, no family, nor anything else without Anthony. He plucked me up nice and ripe, supple young bosom and all. A young, unskilled, naive, and stupid teenager. That is what he wanted in a wife, and that is what he got. And what treasures behold me, should I stay until my last breath? Bleak, forgotten fantasies accompanied by a little bloodshed. The occasional swollen lip, blackened eyes, and perhaps a fracture here and there. What life is one such as this? A life where you pray for your husband's death? *Please God! Give me the strength not to seek a man who would carry out such an evil deed on my behalf.*

He's a little older than me, but age doesn't matter that much. Unless you are like Anna Nicole or something. Until I'm marrying an old geezer who's bedridden and about to kick the bucket, I'm not going to worry about the difference. It's probably about ten years, but since I'm not going to care about age, I'm not even going to ask him. Just looking at Tee, I can tell he's young at heart. Anyone with a sly grin like that has skeletons in the closet, though. Children keep secrets because they're naughty and don't want to get caught. I know a ton of adults that never outgrew that trait, yet somehow everyone knows everything about everyone around them. My coworkers blab and spread rumors to anyone who will listen. This person is fucking her. This person is fucking him. This person wants to fuck you. Blah, blah, blah. My sister used to say that murderers live by the 3-S rule, and every single one of them gets caught because they forget about the third S: shoot, shovel, and SHUT UP! People just can't help themselves.

I may swear off interoffice relationships forever just because of A & A. I mean, do you know what it is like to go to a company event and see your boss with his wife, but he's staring at his girlfriend over cheap, previously frozen burgers? So there he is eyeing his fling and in the next breath, he questions why his wife is diddling the plumber. The boss's side piece, of course, shows up with a serious piece of eye candy on her arm so that her married "boyfriend" doesn't think her calendar revolves around him. All of this trouble just because he pops a boner for her every now and then. Both women should leave him if you ask me. Wrap your nasty paws around it, and take care of that bone yourself, you dog!

CHAPTER 3

Well, Anthony finally came home this morning to get ready for a day at the office. He asked me if I made him breakfast as if I was expecting him after being MIA for so long. I was just swallowing the last bit of my meal when I told him to go make his own food.

"It feels like every time I exert effort over the stove, my hard work ends up all over the floor," I explained, defiantly.

He chuckled a little and said he would see me after work "probably late." That last bit is no surprise. I really cannot figure out why he finds it necessary to even inform me of his delay at this point. After being gone for three days? In recent years, work has always come before me. I suppose I've always taken a back seat to his career, now that I think back to those lonely days on our honeymoon. Not that I mind it so much anymore. He treats his work with respect and speaks of it with pride. I cannot remember the last time my husband was proud of me or our relationship.

On a brighter note, however, a nice young lady came into the store the other night. She was looking for art instruction, and I could tell she had extremely low self-confidence but such passion about the subject. Maybe that is just the balance of emotions that she needed because she brought a few of her paintings into the store today, and I thought they were absolutely splendid. We made plans for a lunch date so I can take a look at a few more of them. If the others are as good as the couple I saw, I am going to inquire about having a little gallery put up at the bookstore to see if they could sell. I've not yet told her my idea, for I am positive it would crush her spirits if my general manager will not even entertain it. I will wait to see how this all plays out. She is supposed to be here at half-past two. I have a bit of a nervous stomach about having company after so many years of hiding my life from everyone around me.

Tee was wonderful, charming, and witty... and loaded! I'm telling you, he was pulling stacks out of his pocket. Not dollars at all. Fifties, hundreds, and a few twenties. He's a lawyer. Imagine that! We can date, he can buy me all kinds of things, and I'll be doted on like never before. Someday, he'll propose and give me a really gorgeous ring, and he'll wink just like he did when we first met. We'll go on our honeymoon, probably to somewhere in Europe, and I will become the jet-setter I always imagined myself to be. I'll be a famous artist, and he'll be a big-time lawyer for the rich and famous. He'll be like Johnny Cochran, only he'll fight for the prosecution. We can be a power couple. And then we'll have children: one boy and one girl, of course. And we'll live happily ever after, *obviously*. Okay, okay. I don't really believe all of that, but I still can't wait to see him again. He's taking me to dinner tomorrow night. I'll have to make sure I don't drink too much because I might start talking about love at first sight or something else that might scare him away (like planning out our whole life together or some stupid shit like that).

First things first, though. I have to get my paintings together for lunch at Sandra's (the lady from Binded Books who looked at my paintings.) She acted like she genuinely thought they were good, but she might have just been saying that to be nice. Anyway, she invited me for lunch and said she's modest about everything except her cooking which she described as wonderful. She gave me directions to her house. It is in a very nice neighborhood, and I will just assume that she's not a crazy murderer or anything. I hope. I shared my location with Claire just in case. While I'm there, maybe I can figure out why she seems so damn sad. I don't know how I can see it but I totally can. It's like we have some kind of deeper connection or something.

Tiffany is an outstanding spirit. We clicked right away and, better yet, her paintings are beyond magnificent. The colors, the subjects, the sheer meaningfulness of it all. She's a born artist who never bred herself of it. I was amazed, to say the least, that this was the first attempt she's made at her gift. After she left, I immediately called Ray. He is the general manager at Binded Books, and he thought it was a fabulous idea to have a little gallery showing of an "up and coming" artist. He's going to view her work tonight, and we will all meet at Caesar's tomorrow evening for Ray's decision about her work. I know that Tiffany is seeing someone tomorrow night, but I hope she does not brush off this opportunity for a long night with someone she barely knows. It's certainly none of my concern if she wants to go that route on their first date, but she does seem a bit naive about the whole thing.

That dreamy look in her eyes can only be compared to how I felt the hours before Anthony took me out for the first time. Times have changed a bit, I suppose. I would have never considered going further than a peck on the cheek after the first meeting with a man. My cheeks flushed brightly after even such a small gesture like that, and I ran up to my room and flopped onto my bed in blissful delight. My mother came in after she heard my pounding footsteps and, seeing the stupid grin painted across my face, told me that everyone is naive, especially young women such as myself. It felt so insulting at the time, but I completely agree with her today.

"It does not simply go away with age, darling. It exists forever in some, particularly in those that do not learn the value of their mistakes. You will know when you are no longer this naive young lady. Someday, your mistakes will become few and far between. You will realize that you no longer have to make them in order to learn your lessons. Other people will make them, and you will learn from their losses."

It is only eight o'clock, but I am ready for bed. It will be better if I am sleeping when Anthony gets home. I'll not have an opportunity to ask him where he disappeared to for a few days, and that will spare both of us the upset; additionally, it would seem as if I care about his absence, and I emphatically do not. Rather, I feel a small twinge of curiosity. He probably slept at his office. I am not going to ask him. No, sir. I enjoyed myself while he was away and would not mind at all if it became a regular occurrence. I think it's better I keep that last bit to myself as well. It's best not to insult my husband.

Sandra's house was nice and all, but something was off. It was decorated in such an impersonal way. It reminded me of an upscale hotel lobby. It was pretty, but it didn't really have the feeling of an actual "home." Everything was picture perfect... except for the pictures, that is. There were no pictures of family on the walls, nor even of friends. I know that Sandra and her husband don't have any kids, but there weren't even pictures of the two of them. Not even so much as a single wedding photograph. There were wonderful paintings of people and beautiful photos of some landscapes – places they visited in younger years, perhaps? – but it seemed a little weird. Shouldn't the smiling faces that beam down from their walls be of actual, real-life people? They are covered in fiction, thought up by artists, and sold at auction. Sandra came from someone's womb, so why aren't there any pictures of her mother? Does she have siblings? When I first got to the house, she seemed a little distracted, but she appeared to relax after a few minutes.

That familiar sadness just about disappeared from her eyes. Just about.

It was indescribable but I'll try my best: cooking a nice meal and having someone there to appreciate it was something akin to a miracle. It was so delightful to have Tiffany over for lunch. I threw together a colorful springtime pasta to lighten my mood, and it definitely worked. The ingredients looked so beautiful when combined: green beans; red, orange, and yellow peppers; and white feta cheese. What a delightful, cheerful dish. I think it has extended my good mood, and I am incredibly grateful for that. Anything that gives me a swift kick towards happiness is a wonderful thing. This easy, one-pot, springtime pasta is certainly on my list as comfort food. I do not like to use food as a vice for my emotions, but I will allow them to lighten my mood or make a bad day a little better. Not the same thing, in my opinion.

"When you are down, do not eat food to feel better. Find that strength in the people around you and, with them, share your comfort food over healing conversation." My mother, ever the teacher.

For the past few years, I have not really found strength in conversation with anyone (not even with myself.) Until Tiffany, that is. I have a friend now. One friend. It has taken me so long to find that in another being. The bond between two females is something quite sacred, and I had all but forgotten what it felt like. To talk of love and losses; to talk, period. I imagine the prospect of having only one friend would cause most women sadness. I, however, am as giddy as the night of my first date. With a swell of newfound pride, I think of her. With hopefulness, I pray for this friendship to grow into a bond that offers both of us strength and confidence in the areas we are weak. *Please, God. Give me one healthy relationship with another human being. Just one.*

I have to meet Tee tonight at six o'clock, and I don't get out of this hellhole until five. We're going to a place called Mr. G's. It's supposed to be the best restaurant in town. You have to park valet, and the waiters light your cigarettes and pulls your chair out for you. I should smoke tonight just for fun. Just kidding!

Mostly kidding.

Claire's boyfriend/baby daddy works there, and he said that the average price for two people to eat dinner is like $350! What the hell am I supposed to wear to a place like that?

"Something sexy, not slutty," my friend advised. Thank you, Claire, for your heartfelt and oh-so-specific advice. I'm serious, though. That is almost what I make in a week. Thanks, Bob. Thank you for paying me the wonderful amount of jack shit! It's not even worth the little amount of money I make, either. Today, he wouldn't stop staring at my tits. Every time he would talk to me, his gaze would repeatedly dart to my chest and, eventually, they just never came back to make eye contact again.

"Tiffany, would you mail this for me?"

"Tiffany, would you fax this right away?" NOT looking at my face.

Finally, I couldn't stand it anymore. "Sorry, Bob, are you confused? My breasts are never actually going to reply, no matter how much you babble to them."

"I just really like your shirt, Tiff. Very nice design." And he walked away, completely unphased, just like that. He couldn't find *anything* better to say? What a basic, little man. Claire ran into her office and slammed the door, she was laughing so hard.

"I can't believe you said that to him. You are nuts!" She shut her door quickly and shrieked at me as soon as I walked into her office later that afternoon.

I laughed and questioned her, "What's he going to do, fire me? I really don't think he would have the balls to fire either one of us, no matter what we said to him. Do you? What a schmuck."

"You're right about that," she chuckled again. "We're office candy to him!"

Then we started to talk about how this company is so damn weird. Everyone is having an affair with someone else in the office. I'm sure other offices don't operate this way. No way in hell. Bob cheated on his present wife (while she was pregnant) with his secretary. The wife had his baby and stayed with him because of that cha-ching, I can only assume. Before they were married, though, his current wife was his housekeeper. That's right, folks, he cheated on his first wife to bang the maid. Common sense would tell you that if they cheat to be with you, they will probably cheat on you. His first wife left him for his best friend. Paybacks are a bitch, aren't they? Bob's sister, Becky, works for A & A as the lawyer/head of HR. Instead of Human Resources, it should stand for "horny relations." She's hella nasty, too. A chemist on staff didn't knock before walking into her office one day, and he got more than an eyeful! Becky and one of the sales representatives, Steve, were going at it right on top of her desk. Yuck, yuck, yuck! Becky and Steve are both married, too. The list goes on and on. Plant supervisors, customer service representatives, everyone. I don't get it. I'd say fifty percent of our married coworkers cheat on their spouses while they are at work. This, of course, is just a rough estimation Claire and I came up with. It's not a scientific calculation. It's just a loose (no pun intended) guess based on the number of skanky whores we work with.

I poked my head into her door the other day, "I'm telling you, Claire. Bob just doesn't pay us enough green to run the risk of seeing Big Becky giving Steve a blowjob!" I feigned throwing up a little and then left for the day without telling Becky I was through. Technically, she's my boss, so I have to tell her when I'm leaving. But her door was closed, and walking in on some nasty shit like that is not what I am getting paid for. Anyway, I'm just pretending to work right now. Why am I even here? As long as they see a look of concentration on my face and a pen moving, I don't think they even care. If Steve still gets a salary while getting neck, I can make a grocery list.

Oh, fuck me! It's five o'clock already! I've done pretended my way to the end of the day, and I have to go get ready for my date. Claire lives right by the office, and she's my sounding board, so I'm going over to her house before I meet Tee. Ahhhh, I'm so excited!

Last night Anthony came home from the office, crawled into bed next to me, and gave me a tender kiss on the lips. He took me in his arms and made sweet love to me. We have not had this level of intimacy in years. There was actual "cuddling" afterward, and we fell asleep entwined in each other's limbs. It has been forever since we fell asleep embracing. At first, a part of me thought it was a dream, as this reality ended some time ago. In the beginning, we had a loving relationship. Well, that's how I perceived it, at least.

As the grogginess of morning subsided, I saw my husband's age come into focus. The fine lines in his face and around his eyes were telltale signs that this was not merely a dream. I would like to think our few days apart had some good effect on us and that maybe he has changed a bit, but I absolutely refuse the notion. I will never be naive again. I have learned a lot through my years with Anthony and one night of passion, no matter how lovely, cannot erase how much pain he has caused me in these last fifteen years. I admit, a part of me would like to be young again and think this nightmare is over, but I fear it is just beginning. Now that I've lost my temper, I feel unhinged. It absolutely worries me. What if I lose my inhibitions again?

The first three years with my husband flew by. They were filled with countless moments of pure bliss, from my perspective. Sure, we didn't see each other much, but when we did, the good outweighed the bad. From four years on, however, my home life has been a whirlwind of misery, a constant downward spiral. I have lost all of my friends and family. I have sunk into the depths of a deep depression that countless women have lived in. Digging myself out of those dark holes of mental isolation was the hardest thing in the world. It seemed so much easier to check out completely, just sitting in front of the television to sulk. Sometimes I didn't even bother to turn it on first. Staring at a blank screen, I would wonder when all of the hurt would go away. *Does it ever really end?* I still ask, questioning if the pain would be present if Anthony were suddenly gone. *You'll never know, you silly girl.*

Will you never learn?

Just in the last few weeks, my life has shown such improvement. Working at Binded is better than ever because it is the time of year when we do inventory which, to me, is a fun and different task. I am very excited to help Tiffany promote her artwork, pending Ray's decision tonight, and I am starting to want to socialize. This is the point where my pessimistic side typically takes over. If I feel like I am going uphill in this battle called life, who is going to try to push me back down next? If it is not my husband, I will be shocked. I know that every time I taste a little bit of nectar from the fruits of happiness, he is the worm waiting inside to cause me to vomit. I am so mad now. It is sickening. How did I let this happen? Why does he get to me so damn much? I try to untwist myself from his tight muscular morning embrace, suddenly completely disgusted with myself.

I have looked in the mirror no less than 7,000 times in the last 30 minutes to see if I look okay. Claire waxed my brows and curled the back of my hair. Carl took their daughter, Ciera, to the zoo, so now we are just sitting around having a couple of White Claws before it's time for me to meet Tee. About 15 more minutes, and I'm out the door.

Claire thinks Carl is going to propose soon. Guys aren't very good at keeping secrets. The other day, he tried to check her ring size while she was taking a nap next to Ciera. Of course, it woke her up, and he chucked the ring sizer across the bedroom. Subtle as fuck! Now, he keeps bringing up different places, claiming he is "just curious" where her dream vacation would be. I asked her why doesn't she just tell him the truth? That she's not stupid, and it doesn't take a rocket scientist to figure out what his game is. She said if she did that, it would suck all of the fun out of it, and it's better for Carl and his masculinity if she just plays dumb.

"Let him think he's clever," she mumbled with her head practically inside a dresser drawer. She won't tell him she knows, but she is currently obsessed with looking for a ring that may – or may not – exist.

Well, time to go! Deep breaths. Take a couple, and hope for the best. If worse comes to worst, I can leave the date and go to Caesar's early for my meeting with Sandra and her boss. I will write more later about that exciting opportunity. I'm honestly so relieved to have a last-minute commitment after my date tonight.

What am I doing? Am I really trying to convince another individual that I could have a positive influence on their life? This is a joke. My life is a complete sham. How am I supposed to help someone improve when, at the same time, I have been on a steady decline for so many years?

I just had dinner with Tee, and it was magical. He is sooo adorable and delicious. Although, I'm not sure you can accurately describe someone in his mid-thirties as "adorable." What's in an age where there's love? Not that I really *love* him after our first date, but if he is half the gentleman that he has been, it won't be long before I do.

Even more exciting was what happened before my

amazing date, and I didn't get a chance to write about it before leaving. Just as I was walking out the door of A & A Chemicals to go to Claire's, Sandra called and asked if I could meet her and her boss, Ray, at Caesar's at nine o'clock. She wouldn't tell me exactly what was going on, but she said to bring a couple of my paintings, so I knew it had to do with that. At first, she just said she wanted me to meet her boss.

"I know I complain about my job a lot, Sandra, but I don't think that I said that much about it in the short time we've known each other!"

She started laughing, "You're hilarious, Tiffany! I am not getting you a job at Binded. Just bring some of your artwork, okay? Please? I'm so excited about this surprise!"

"No worries, I'll see you then. I have to leave for my date with Tee. Wish me luck!"

She confirmed, "See you at nine o'clock. And good luck, not that you need it."

"On the dot," I assured her. Sandra didn't sound very good today. I'm sure she'll be better tonight, though. I hope. She's probably just tired or something. She told me they're doing inventory at her store. Sounds awful if you ask me.

CHAPTER 4

When I left for Caesar's, Anthony still had not graced me with his presence. He is probably at his precious office still – not that it's a surprise, in the least. I arrived at 8:30 to have a glass of White Zinfandel to calm my nerves. I am as giddy regarding Tiffany's artwork as I once was about my writing. She has so many wonderful experiences to look forward to in her life. If I can help her get out of her dead-end job to pursue something more enjoyable – something meaningful she is truly passionate about – I have made a real difference in someone's life. I am terrified to witness anyone journey down the path I have gone down. I don't want her to end up in my position, lost and alone, abused, and full of regret. I feel like I went to sleep one night with aspirations of greatness, longing to make an impact on the world around me, only to open my eyes a decade later wondering where it went awry. I wasn't sure what happened to the daydreaming girl I once knew in myself. In my younger years, I was quite the spunky individual. Hard to believe now, looking at me. Now, I am practically invisible. I am adamant about helping Tiffany find the right path for herself. I need Spunky Sandra to make her appearance. She's been absent way too long.

The Path to Utopia

Sometimes long, sometimes short
   No matter the length of your stride
It may seem calm or equally difficult
   Depends on the measures you try
Trust and believe, but leave your heart
   Both hindsight and blinding myopia
Lofty dreams are worth the result
   Oh, treacherous path to Utopia.

My only utopia is this journal. Even though I am not a published author, I still consider myself a writer, of sorts. As long as I am writing, I will always be what I once was. And as long as I'm breathing, I'll continue to write. My wine has arrived, and I do have priorities in place this evening, so this little notebook will get stashed away soon. I can pretend I am normal and happy for a few moments. *I hope.*

My thanks to the young bartender and his mesmerizing blue eyes. If he could sing, he might be able to pull himself off as the new Frank Sinatra. We could refer to him as "Young Blue Eyes." I supposed he's a little too young to like music that dated, and I wonder if he would even understand my reference. Then again, I'm too young for my own reference, I think humorously to myself.

Tonight, when I met up with Tee, it suddenly hit me that he looks super familiar. I could almost swear I have seen him before, but I can't place where. Maybe I didn't notice when we first met because it was a short conversation, and the lights at Caesar's are on the dim side. After spending a couple of hours together, his mannerisms seemed eerily familiar to me. There was nothing at all threatening in his tone of voice or actions but once, when he moved, I flinched a little. It surprised me. Maybe I was zoning. Claire complains that I zone a lot. She'll be talking and I won't even hear her, but I still manage to say all the right things in all the right places. Only later, when I'm confused, will she complain that I'm always in my own head. She's not wrong. I'll just write it off as a character flaw on my side. After all, the date was absolutely perfecto in every way!

If there is one thing my mother wouldn't be caught dead with, it's a glass of White Zin. The one and only time I remember her getting too tipsy to function was from White Zinfandel wine. She was positively mortified the day after her drunken stupor. Loud and obnoxious slurred talking, cackling laughter, and sharing stories she'd rather have kept private. It was enough for her to swear off white wine for life.

"The definition of insanity is to repeat a behavior over and over expecting different results. I am a sane woman. Always have been and always will be. Perhaps it was a temporary sanity paralysis that grabbed hold, and I'll be damned if I ever lose control of my wits again in this lifetime. So help me God, I will never have another drink for the rest of my days if I'm ever caught in public even half as drunk as that evening."

She had a look of determination and defiance in her eyes like she was staring down the devil himself. Perhaps she was – I never asked her. All I know is that I have never seen my mother have more than two drinks in one sitting, and she's likely still kept her word to this day. *If she is still alive.*

To the core of my being, I hope someday to again hear her wise advice. Sure, I hear from an impersonation inside my own thoughts. I suppose that is better than nothing at all. If only in my thoughts, at least she is present. Hopefully, her memory will live forever, sustaining me throughout this painful life she disagrees with. Until the day I leave my husband or meet my demise, that sweet imaginary voice will have to do.

I went to Caesar's to meet Sandra and her boss, Ray. I brought three of my favorite paintings including the one I got mad about and ripped up. I'm glad we met at the bar because I got to show Tom my stuff. I thought he would hate them or make fun, but he didn't act like that at all. He actually seemed impressed. I'm starting to wonder if I'm more than a little attracted to him. Those eyes of his are beyond incredible.

But Tee... Tee is so magical. I would say the first date is too soon to tell, but we totally clicked. There was an undeniable and instant spark of chemistry between us, that's for sure. But enough of this crush talk. I got fantastic news today. Literally, I got the best news ever!

What a great day, seriously. First, I got to spend time with Claire sans her child. Don't get me wrong, I love Ciera to death, but it's just not the same around a mom when she has her kid under her feet. Then came my awesome date with Tee where we dined on caviar and drowned ourselves in expensive wine. I ate a lot of food I honestly still can't pronounce, so I'm happy he ordered for me. And the best part of the whole evening is that Ray saw my paintings, loved them, and he wants me to price them and have a little gallery thing at Binded Books.

"SHUT UP!" I exclaimed. "WHAT? Are you for real?" I am so beyond stoked about this opportunity, but I feel like I have an itsy-bitsy problem: I have no idea how to price my work. I expressed my concerns, and he said to think about it and give him a call when I figure it out. He acted like it was no big deal that I don't know what I'm doing *at all*. This is happening because of Sandra. I'm still in disbelief that she orchestrated this for me. I mean, I might not even sell anything, but this is such a dream.

Ray handed me his business card before he left us, and I felt like a real adult for once. I'm so used to being treated like shit at A & A. I'm kinda overwhelmed by all of the kindness I'm being shown. When I didn't know how to paint, I went to Binded to read up on it. Now I'm over here trying to figure out how to price my artwork. Wow, life is crazy unpredictable. I guess I'll be hitting up the bookstore after work tomorrow.

Gah! I can't wait to tell Claire!

I saw it in her entire face and clear as day, that poor girl. She's falling for that older businessman so fast and after only one date, too. I also spied something else, though. Tiffany and that handsome, young bartender at Caesar's were definitely flirting with each other. Do they even realize their attraction? He seems like such a nice young man and quite handsome. Shaggy blond hair and those entrancing baby blues. His eyes remind me of how my husband's used to look. They were so full of life. I can tell that Tiffany is full of life as well. Her spirit is so uplifting, so light. It makes me feel a little better today, thinking of the way her face lit up at Caesar's.

And after what happened last night when I got home, I need any kind of pick-me-up that life has to offer. Anthony and his friend, Jack Daniels, were sitting on the couch waiting for me. I could tell he'd been drinking for at least a couple of hours. I tried to quietly pass him to go into the kitchen but "tried" and "accomplished" are two entirely different results. Needless to say, I didn't make it to my destination as I'd hoped. Even after almost a fifth of Jack – if that's *all* he consumed – he is much quicker and more adept in swift movements than I am. He had me pinned against the wall in an instant, the near-empty bottle dangling from his left hand and my throat tightly grasped with his dominant right. He started shaking me and was screaming so loud that, ironically, I couldn't really catch what he was actually saying. Piercing volume erupted from his enraged face, full of uncontrollable anger.

What choice do I have but to wait out this madness? With as much patience as I was able to muster, I submit. The more you fight it, the longer it lasts, and the more it hurts. He knew I was not at work, so what must he think of my absence at such a late hour as this? Anthony writes my schedule for Binded on the kitchen wall calendar. There was no point in telling him where I was. You cannot reason with an unreasonable man, and I've very little freedom afforded to me outside of work.

I have to believe God has a plan for everyone. Will I finally realize my life's purpose when I unleash the wisdom locked deep inside of myself? Will I ever be rewarded for my good deeds and pure heart? After I'm suddenly and unexpectedly freed from his grip, I stumble to my room to see if I've got a turtleneck to wear for work tomorrow. Thank God it's cooler weather right now so I'm able to easily hide any marks. I'm so relieved when I find I have several options laundered and available. Life is all about cherishing the small blessings.

I have a dream. I know it's a famous line, but I've never been able to use it. I've never felt like there was one thing I could do for the rest of my life to earn a living. Maybe I just didn't know until now that it was really a possibility. I wonder if some people don't figure out their purpose until they're 30, 40, or even 50 years old. I'm sure there are tons of people that retire from a job they never liked but, for one reason or another, felt obligated to stay at. Then, they realize they've spent the majority of their days unsatisfied after finding their true passion. Do they feel excited or regretful in their realization? Would they pursue that newfound passion or assume it was now too late? What if they decided it was too late and then lived to be 100? At half of their life, they just gave up on their dreams, and for what? To continue living an unfulfilled life. That probably happens a lot. I won't do that. I refuse to waste my dreams. Our talents are gifts and meant to be shared with the world around us.

Claire is literally such a good friend. She is being so great and supportive about everything. She is so positive about life and says stuff like:

"Ohhhh, I'm so happy for you!"

"I'm sure you'll sell something, probably all of it!"

"Tee sounds dreamy!"

"I know everything will work out, so stop worrying."

She builds up my confidence whenever I feel it's lacking. I'm finally getting my shit together. If I ever become a renowned artist and make a lot of money, I'm going to get Claire something really nice. Even if I don't talk to her anymore after I leave A & A, I would love to do something really significant for her. I mean, I hope we still talk. We should keep in touch, but you never know what life will bring so who knows? I'm going to invite her to Caesar's tonight. Whether she can get a sitter (or if Carl will be home to stay with CeeCee) is what dictates Claire's schedule. Ciera is seriously one of the cutest kids I've ever seen. She's got curly blonde hair and deep blue eyes that must've been borrowed from a porcelain doll or something. She is super petite, just like Claire, but they don't look alike in any other way at all. Claire's family is full-blooded Italian. Her mom and all of her sisters have the same olive skin, black hair, and dark eyes. Carl is like a fucking albino in comparison! Of course, he's not really, but you know what I mean. His genes must be so strong because Ciera got almost all of his features.

Anyway, CeeCee is sooo adorable, but I still hope her mom can get out of the house and away from her tonight. I'm sure one of her four sisters could watch her if Carl refuses. I just hate when dads won't stay home once in a while to take care of their own damn kids so mom can get out to have a night of fun. Who do they think they are, anyway? He gets to have "guy time" really often, so why does my girl always have to bend over backward to try to find a sitter? Girls night out STAT, I demand it!

Not that Carl is one of these guys all the time, so I shouldn't even be complaining. Especially since I don't even have kids yet. I don't know how it feels to live in their shoes. He did take CeeCee to the zoo the other day, but I don't know. It still seems imbalanced to me. In reality, I'm just talking a bunch of smack because I want to go out with my friend tonight. We hardly ever hang out without the baby. That mom life! It seems like a hard gig to balance. I could stand to wait a few more years before I'm tied down, that's for sure. I'm either selfish or smart. Maybe a little of both.

When I got to work today, Tiffany was already waiting for me to arrive. She said that a lot of workers were willing to help her, but she was embarrassed by the fact that she didn't know how to price her artwork, and she was too self-conscious to tell them the truth.

I advised, "The only thing to be embarrassed about when knowledge needs to be sought is not going to look for it. Here you are, so there you go. You've already won half the battle." She said she felt comfortable asking me. *Comfortable.* My heartstrings have been tugged from such a simple concept. I hope I can feel this way someday. I yearn for the freedom to express what goes on in my other life, the one filled with hate and anger and pain. I haven't been able to talk to anyone for so long about what my home life is about. Sometimes I wish I could die in that secret life and completely thrive in this one. This one with work, friends, and the facade of happiness. I think of the painful bruises hiding below my burgundy shirt and squirm uncomfortably. I can only hope to die in my other life. Sadly, to obtain such a privilege is impossible. If I die there, I die here as well. For the time being, I will attempt to shine brighter while outside of my home, rejoicing that I still have some good to revel in. I know I am fortunate in so many ways that others are not. God knows, it could always be worse.

Tiffany only stayed for a bit because she had to meet a friend at Caesar's. She's meeting someone she works with, from my understanding. It sounds like a dreadful place, a chemical company filled to the brim with sexual harassment, adultery, and lies. At least she has a comrade with whom she can trust and speak with about these problems. From her stories, the harassment is not only her burden but also her friend's as well. After we talked over all of this, the artwork conundrum resurfaced and was swiftly resolved.

Well, I've got almost all of my paintings priced and framed, and I'm feeling very good about this whole gallery situation. Of course, Sandra has a lot to do with it. That, and the fact that Claire and I went to Caesar's last night and had such a rad time. We got completely trashed off of Long Island iced teas. I remembered Tom had made a joke about Tee the first time we met. I'd never had one, and that drink fucked my whole entire world up after just a few. Strongest drink ever! I never told Claire that I was kind of thinking about Tom being cute and all, but she must have known because she embarrassed the shit out of me.

When he was bringing over our third (and final) drinks, Claire slurred, "Tiffany lubs youuu!" Tom looked at me and smiled with a something in his eyes that I'd never seen before. Then, Claire started laughing and pointing, "Look, Tom lubs Tiffany, too." This was followed by the beginning of her singing, "Tiffy n Tommy sitting in a –"

THUD Instead of Claire saying "tree," she fell off her barstool.

"Who falls off a barstool with a back, Claire?" I asked between fits of laughter. Tom and I were cracking up. I called us a rideshare shortly after her tumble.

Before I went to Caesar's, I went to Binded to talk to Sandra about pricing my paintings. Thank God she had some advice, "Just how you painted them – with feeling – is how they should be priced. Look at every one of them like you're seeing them for the first time. Rate how strongly each individual painting tugs at your heart and price them according to the strength of the pull."

Sandra is so wise.

CHAPTER 5

This morning, I made breakfast for Anthony, and he was surprisingly appreciative. Actually, he was quite charming, thankful, receptive, talkative, and smiling. I suppose this should make me happy, right? It should be a welcomed change, yes? I cannot allow that, not for one moment. It only leaves me extra nervous, as it practically guarantees it will be a further fall from grace the next time he loses his temper. When he is fleetingly pleasant, I constantly remind myself about the level of evil he is capable of achieving. I try not to do things to set him off and, so far as this morning went, I was successful. But my fearful thoughts are frequent as the day drags on, and he is becoming more agitated by the hour. I recognize the familiar flicker of hatred in his eyes and am able to pinpoint the precise moment he changes into that monster. Sometimes I wonder. *Will this be the time he takes it too far? This could be the time you don't wake up.* I'm not scared, though. No, I've never been afraid of *that* way out. I halfheartedly welcome it, actually.

Okay. I haven't heard from Tee since our date, but he gave me his work cell and instructed me to call, so I decided to just go for it. At first, I was a little nervous, but it ended up being great. We chatted for a few minutes and his landlines were blowing up, so he said he had to go.

Actually, what he said was, "Listen, sweetie, I'm swamped. Meet at Caesar's at 7:00." But I told him no. Yeah, right! Of course, I'm going to meet him. I didn't even give it a second thought. He is so yummy, and I love a man who knows exactly what he wants.

I am greatly looking forward to Tiffany's gallery at the bookstore. So much so, in fact, that it has inspired me to consider pursuing some long-overdue dreams of my own. I picked up a flyer at the market regarding a certain annual poetry contest I have had my eye on for years. True, I haven't written competitively in a while. Nay, in over a decade, really. Surely it's like riding a bike. Perhaps I will enter. Maybe.

On the other hand, it doesn't seem like something that would end well for me. Anthony would not approve. Perhaps, he doesn't have to find out. I'm not fond of deception, but I could use Tiffany's address if I really needed to hide it. I don't know that they would even send any physical mail. How would I even explain the need to her? I certainly don't want to burden my friend, but I do know she would want me to have this opportunity, should I decide to enter. It's really not feasible to believe my husband is at all capable of being supportive, and if he found out of this deceit, well – I simply must use a different address, that's all there is to it.

Can you imagine? This time last year, I wouldn't have even thought about picking up that flyer, let alone entering. It barely caught my eye for more than a moment one short year ago. At that time, I was walking around in a haze. If I flip back through my journal from that period, it is painful to relive. I was in such a deep state of depression (it comes and goes) and every entry oozed with talk of death. I am better now. *Better enough, at least.* Things are definitely looking up. And who knows? I may just win that contest.

Claire is a good friend to me, but I'm afraid we won't talk after we're no longer coworkers. It's not like I don't plan on keeping in touch or anything. It's just that I have jumped around from job to job since I was fourteen years old, and I know not to make promises anymore. When life changes, sometimes it's not easy staying friends forever. Exchanging necklaces engraved with "BFF" are symbols of youthful expectations and full of well-intended lies. I remember having really great friends at my first job, and I am sure we all *meant* to stay connected through the years, but that idea was lost as quickly as it was born. Here's the thing, though: would we even get along with each other now? It's been 9 years, almost a decade. We were only children, and now we are grown. I always rationalize things I should feel guilty for.

But should I even feel guilty? And WHY? Because I'm not the greatest at keeping in touch? It does bother me sometimes that I never called Erin, Marsha, or Beth but at a certain point it feels – well, pointless. It becomes insulting if you don't call someone for five years and then, out of the blue, you're like, "Hi! What are you up to?" It just doesn't work that way. The social aspects of being human legit have me feeling awkward sometimes. Big facts.

If you weren't around last year during their miscarriage or the year before when they watched their mother lose a long battle with cancer, what the hell are you really calling for now? Do you want to know what I am doing? TOO BAD. You gave up that privilege years ago. So, basically, I don't call them because I am scared. How would I feel if they said all of those things to me?

"Where were you when I was hurting?"

Or "We weren't even *really* friends."

And the worst one would definitely be "Wait. Tiffany who?"

So, I really *should* keep in touch with Claire after neither of us works at A & A anymore. I truly care about her, and I don't want to lose her friendship the way I have lost so many others. But her life is so full, balancing work and a family. I wish I wasn't such a job-hopper. I think my patience is almost gone for Bob and my position at A & A Chemicals.

I have had such a lovely evening. Even though I was not very optimistic this afternoon, I found a certain peace after writing. This is not uncommon after journaling; however, today felt different. Tiffany called me from work to tell me about Tee, and I feel content being a confidant for her joyfulness. I would not have called a man first, but I am incredibly inexperienced and was married far too young. Friendship is in bloom, and it has brought me great comfort I had all but forgotten existed in life. I expressed this and told her that she brings me such happiness that I've not found in many years. She thanked me with such concern in her tone, it was practically palpable through our wireless connection that something has her worried. Only now can I truly understand the outdated slogan, "Reach out and touch someone." Maybe I'm not as good as I imagined at feigning happiness.

A few new and ridiculous comments from the balding pervert today.

"You sure do dye your hair a lot, Tiffany." He snickers, and I look at him through narrowed, evil eyes. "Your boyfriend must feel like he's sleeping with a different woman every night."

I glared at him, "I don't have a boyfriend."

"Well, we should change that, shouldn't we?" *wink, wink*

"You might own the company but trust me when I say you couldn't afford me," I snapped at him, quickly.

He smiled, "Ohhhhh, I like my women feisty!"

I retorted, "And I guess your women like their men short and bald?"

I rushed away, mumbling about some work I needed to take care of, to hide out in Clair's office after that. I've never said anything insulting to him. He is my boss, after all. If I know him, though, our convo only turned him on more. What a sick and twisted, tiny man he is. I feel nauseous just thinking about his disgusting comments. While I was in Claire's office, I couldn't resist dishing about my date.

"Did I have a good time with Tee? Yes. Did he kiss me? Yes. Were there huge fireworks and major chemistry? Yes and yes! EEEEEKKK!"

She was laughing and making fun of my smitten disposition. I reminded her of the bar stool incident and pretended to fall off of the chair in her office. I was just joking, and she knows that. I told her all about how Tee bought all of my drinks and fancy food. He complimented me all night long, and we had a wonderful conversation about, well – does conversation really matter that much? The super important part is when he brushed my hair back from my cheek, and I saw this look in his eyes that just made me melt. I love that. If only I were standing at the time, I bet my foot would've popped up during our kiss. *sigh*

His kisses made the butterflies in my midsection intensify. If they were fluttering before, they took full flight after Tee's lips touched mine. *If we get married someday*, I thought, *would the wedding kiss feel this way?* I would hope so! I don't want a marriage that loses spark.

There was just one thing that was kinda irksome. He kept asking me about where I lived and who I lived with. It was almost like he wanted me to invite him over. I felt like he could tell I tensed up the last time he hinted so that ended that. I'm not trying to have him over this soon after meeting, obviously. I've dated a ton of assholes, and I am done dealing with the drama and bullshit that comes with moving too fast. He's going to have to wait until I'm ready. He has no choice. I just don't trust him yet. We barely just met.

I try my best to keep my head up, to always see the silver lining around this cloud we call life, but it is becoming quite the challenge as of late. I am out of work for a bit. Leave of absence is the only way to hide the *literal* shame on my face. Shame can rear its ugly head in many forms and, unfortunately, mine arrives with visible bruises.

Anthony was absolutely insane when he came home last night. I was in bed, nearly asleep when he wanted to have sex. It seemed like such a chore at the time, so I mumbled my halfhearted denial of his request. I could have complied. *I should have complied.* Honestly, I would have gladly obliged, had I known the consequences.

He hurled me onto the floor without warning, and it felt confusing in the half-slumber state I was in. My face hit the carpet, hands flailing in a last-second attempt at self-preservation. He grabbed part of my pale pink nightshirt and yanked me forcefully to my feet. My nose was already bleeding, yet we'd only just begun. My eyes stung with the threat of tears, as I tasted the blood that trickled over my quivering lips. I was slammed against the wall, took several blows to the face, and forcefully tossed like a rag doll back onto our bed where it had all started.

Our bed? No, no. That is inaccurate. It leads one to believe we share a partnership of some sort. He ripped off my underwear and proceeded to have painful and forceful intercourse with me. My muscles were tense from the shock and horror, and it made it hurt more than it should for someone who has been married for so long. I looked up at my husband through my swollen eyes and ran my tongue over my split lip. *I will not cry for this disgusting excuse of a man. Never again, this I vow.* There wasn't even a sliver of hope in those cold, black eyes of his. He must've felt my thoughts because he looked me square in my face and smacked me. Hard.

The absolute realization that this is what I've allowed my life to become stung much more than my cheek. How have I been so lost for so many years? Can I even find my way back to the hopeful girl I once was? She seems dead today. Gone. These thoughts screamed loudly as my husband violently raped me. Is this the closest I will come to understand the pain of bearing a child? Blood sprayed and showered the air, staining the white satin sheets. I gripped them tightly in my clenched fists and bit the inside of my jaw to fight against the pain that ripped through my vagina.

His vagina, I mentally corrected my verbiage as I slipped into unconsciousness. I welcomed the escape.

Sandra called me at work to tell me she couldn't come to my gallery at the bookstore. What in the actual fuck? She said she would be really busy with "personal matters" and wouldn't have the time to attend, nor be at Binded for a while. Not enough time for a friend? That doesn't sound like the Sandra I know. And she took a personal leave of absence from work? She loves her job, so I am lowkey worried about her now. Something smells fishy.

I know we haven't been friends for very long, but she has helped me so much in the little time since we met. I have always felt we had an instant connection, and I care tremendously about her already. I could see the sadness in her eyes, and I didn't want to pry by asking her questions she may not want to answer, but now I feel like I did her a disservice. I bet whatever caused that look in her eyes is the very thing keeping her "busy" now. Busy, my ass! She is so full of shit. I know this gallery opening is important to her, and I have to find out what is going on. *What are you hiding, my friend?*

I spoke with Tiffany today, and she carried the conversation with such composure when I told her I could not attend her gallery, no matter the date. Of course, she knows something is wrong, but I simply couldn't bring myself to tell her the truth. I am much too ashamed to utter anything even remotely close to the truth.

I know she would flippantly say, "Leave him." Just like that. As if it's a basic task I could accomplish over the course of an afternoon. It's not like it hasn't crossed my mind on countless occasions, but I cannot fathom actually going through with it. I have never gone to college, nor held a full-time job. It is hopeless to think Anthony will ever change – *that he is even capable of change.* Yet, I still dreamt of the day an invisible switch would be triggered, and we could find happiness together... *until now.*

All relationships have their peaks and valleys, even ours. Good times have been had, although few and far between. Those rare moments kept a tiny beacon of light burning inside. Those minuscule glimmers of hope kept me captivated by wishes of our happily ever after. An endless and unfulfilled yearning. Those little whispers and sideways snickers he threw at me on the good days? They're my poison. I lap those moments up like a starved animal, my wild eyes constantly searching him for more. Always waiting for my next fix, his charisma became my drug, but there was never a second helping. Only rations over here. Scraps. Leftovers, at best. Through the years, the good moments started to come at slower intervals. They were so rare that I'd be left feeling sustained for weeks from one slightly pleasant interaction. Sure, we have stretches of time without drama. I wouldn't say they are "good" times, but they aren't all that terrible, either. Mediocracy is a vast improvement over even the nicest offerings of his "bad" days. You would think I would just get used to it. Maybe I will, after another decade or so.

Every time I hear my clothes rip. Every time I cannot breathe. Every time I taste blood in my mouth. So often, it hurts like the first time. Just in the beginning, though. Emotionally, mentally, and physically, the deep-seated pain has never dulled through these years. It just sits down inside me waiting to be unleashed. On the few occasions I've had the privilege of catching a glimpse of myself in the mirror during an attack, I see a contradicting mixture of pure terror and a blank look of hopelessness.

He has all the power. While he is strutting around as the boss, I am tiptoeing on eggshells in constant fear. In our house, I am the prey. The meek little mouse in a snake's cage. It is inevitable that the hunter will pounce, but I never quite know when he will feel his hunger. There is rarely a warning. Before Anthony can kill me, surely this prison of a house will provide my death. Now that I'm out of work, dying of boredom feels like it could be an actual possibility. *Quarantine kills.*

How I wish I could confide in Tiffany. My beautiful friend, Tiffany. *Could I?* NO! What if he found out I told someone what he does to me behind these closed doors? I would live in terror every day for the rest of my life. *But how is that different than how I already live?* No, it is just too dangerous to let anyone into this secret life I lead. As of late, he has been getting worse, and I certainly don't want to jeopardize the one friendship I long to keep hold of.

CHAPTER 6

I've been avoiding the telephone today because I simply do not feel like talking to anyone. I certainly have not minded missing all the telemarketer calls. I don't believe for a moment the "do not call" list actually helps anyone.

"We're calling about the warranty on your vehicle," The computer-generated voice begins.

Or my favorite, "Your social security number has been compromised." Oh no, robot lady! Whatever shall I do to correct this unfortunate event?

It is highly unlikely that Anthony would try to reach me, but I want to be certain not to pick up, should he do so. I've kept my ringer on silent all day. After all, what will he do if I ignore him? Punish me? Who the hell cares anymore? I feel like I am stuck at the bottom of a deep, dark hole in the ground. There is no one to hear my cries, but I'm close enough to see everything I am missing out on above me. When I was a little girl, I thought marriage was like going to live in a real-life fairy tale. My parents had a marriage like that. They always got along, dinner was on the table every night when my father walked in from work, and everyone seemed happy. He was a grateful husband; she was a doting wife. I imagined my childhood household was that of a typical marriage.

I was sadly mistaken. Perhaps their marriage was the exception, not the norm. My discovery of the truth came much too late. My overworked father has been passed for eight years (from an unexpected heart attack), and I have not had a genuine and real conversation with my mother since his passing. When I was notified of my father's death, I was devastated. I tried to talk to my husband about my overwhelming emotions. I was desperate for comfort or some sort of empathy. Something, anything. Stumbling over my words during such a heavy time of despair, I had barely managed to say anything at all when Anthony began raging at me. On the day of my father's funeral, my eye was so bruised and swollen that I could not attend. During our brief call, my mother threw harsh accusations at me for disrespecting such a wonderful man as my father. It was incredibly painful, and she has not spoken to me since that day. She will never know the immense guilt I still feel for not mourning my father in the proper manner. Why did he have to die, yet my husband still lives a comfortable and carefree life? Anthony deserves to be rotting in the deepest pits of hell, yet here he sits.

The gallery is going down tomorrow night which is amazing because Friday is one of Binded Books busiest nights. I'm very nervous but excited as hell! I tried to call Sandra all day. I knew she would have some words of wisdom for me, but all I got was her voicemail.

"You have reached Anthony and Sandra," a much younger version of my friend chirped in the recording. I was going to leave a message expressing my concern but a feeling in my gut stopped me. I could be wrong, but I think something is up with her husband. Why does her voicemail say both of their names, yet she has literally never mentioned him at all? In fact, she has never said anything about the fact that she is even married. If she didn't wear a ring, I wonder if I would've ever known. If I can't get in touch with her this weekend, I'm going to stop by her house Monday. She can't avoid me forever.

Anthony came home from work today and was feeling particularly savage. The amusement reflected in his eyes as he looked at my battered face and told me I was pretty. The humility I felt at that moment was staggering. He forced me to cook his dinner in the nude. With my back to him, I was able to hide any emotion that threatened to bubble over. My tears only serve to feed his satisfaction. Sick fuck will not have that today.

The searing pain traveled from my midsection all the way up to my bloodshot, swollen eyes as grease jumped from the pan in front of me. As I fried up bacon for Anthony's BLT, I lost count of the number of tiny scolds I received. Every *pop* from the pan made my body jump and tense in anticipation. I did not turn away, nor take a single step backward. I continued monitoring the bacon until it was nice and crisp. *Perfection.*

By the time it had finished, I have become desensitized to it anyway. It only hurts at the beginning, remember? We, humans, are structured to adapt. I smiled as I served his sandwich. It was cold and bitter, laced with the promise of vengeance. Did he see it? Probably not. He saw his dinner. He saw another powerful win in whatever game we are playing here. Someday, I will be the one laughing. Revenge is sweet, or so I've heard.

Wait. Am I going insane? I am merely a product of my environment if that's the case. Suffering of my own making. Why could I not see the type of person Anthony was? The person he was to become. What was I supposed to do in response to his ridiculous dinner request, as opposed to obliging to serve him? As he sat there, stinking of whiskey, poking fun of the tiny bits of cellulite on my thighs – not much, but nevertheless – I wept inside. The amount of self-pity was immeasurable at that moment. My heart aches. The pain, so intense, started stirring a fiery ball of resentment deep inside of me. It is becoming a daily struggle to silence the irrational ideas I'm having.

Sanity. What does it mean? To me, it is only the opposite of insane. Webster defines it only as "the quality or state of being sane. E*specially*: soundness or health of mind." Am I not? Does everyone feel a twinge of insanity in life? Surely, not everyone; not my mother. If most people could identify with temporary insanity, does that not become the "new normal?" Who dictates the importance of sanity over insanity anyhow? I live teetering in and out of both. Doesn't everyone, or am I abnormal?

The gallery was a hit, and I had so much fun. I even sold two of my paintings: one was a black, white, and gray abstract for $80.00 and the one with different color trees with a black and white shack for $120. I can't believe I'm two hundred fucking dollars richer than I was at this time yesterday. How crazy! I tried to call Sandra again to tell her about my successful first night, but it didn't even ring and went straight to voicemail this time.

I'm going to swing by her house and see what's up. Today, I have another date with Tee. I could get used to this life, for real. I think I'm going to wear a baby blue shirt, a tight pencil skirt, and the new shoes I bought from part of my profits. The blue shirt goes with my blonde hair and tan skin really well, and I think it really makes my blue eyes pop. Tee has brown eyes. I always joke around with Claire and say that if a person has brown eyes, it's because they're full of shit. Tee doesn't seem like he's full of it, though. Or does he? He's an older, sophisticated, polite gentleman that just happens to be extremely hot! I'm still not going to put out soon, even if he does seem like the perfect man. After all, "perfect" doesn't necessarily mean perfect for me. Claire said I should adhere to the third date rule, but I think that's bunk. Three or thirty, I'll sleep with him whenever I damn well please and not a moment sooner. I'm sure tonight will be unforgettable, with or without sex.

Depression is taking over. Once again, all I do is sit around and sulk. I need to start a project – something to keep my mind off of my despicable existence. If I keep focusing on the pain I feel, both emotional and physical, it will dictate everything I do... which is NOTHING. When I am truly immersed in my depression, it's hard to even get out of bed. I just lay there for long periods of time, too mentally drained for anything.

I have decided to write a book to pull me out of this funk. My book will be about an abusive, alcoholic husband. Sound a bit too familiar? A writer should write about what they know, right? I certainly know enough about how it feels to be abused by the one person who vowed to protect you. I know the love for the man; I know the hatred for the alcoholic. I know the repercussions of glancing at him the "wrong way" or cooking the wrong meal for dinner. I know what it feels like to be raped by your own spouse. I also know I am not the only one. Even if I wrote a fictitious tale, countless other women would identify with it. This "fiction" is a reality for so many. *Too many*. What a traumatic existence to endure.

Talk about a dream date. Last night I felt like a princess. Tee called around noon and asked for directions. He picked me up at two o'clock on the dot, just as he promised. He took me to Brandt Park, and we sat by a picturesque lake as we ate. He went all out for this picnic and brought poached salmon, steamed veggies, and strawberries with pink champagne for dessert.

"Pink is my favorite color," I squealed with delight.

It was a bit cold even with the jacket I brought, per his instruction. He brought blankets for each of us but, in the end, we just snuggled up against one another under one blanket. After our picnic, we went to a Shakespeare festival where they performed Romeo and Juliet. It sounds cliché, but it was really amazing. There were jugglers, dancers, and tons of vendors set up. We passed on the food because we had just eaten, but we did order wine during the play. Afterward, we went to the grocery store to grab dinner before going back to my apartment. He brought a bag in with him. When I asked about it, he gave me a little wink and wouldn't tell me a thing. After he cooked me dinner – yes, HE cooked – I was ordered to go into my room for a few minutes and come out with my eyes closed.

And I was floored when I opened them again. The whole apartment was candlelit. There must've been a hundred candles just in the dining area and living room alone. I've really never seen anything so breathtaking in my whole life. It was all so romantic that it was pretty hard to make him leave in the end. I'm positive he expected to stay the night, but I'm too afraid of being burned again. No pun intended! He doesn't really seem like the type of man who would hurt anyone, but we haven't even talked about being exclusive yet, and that is an important conversation to have. He is so in tune with what a woman is looking for in a man. Is it real or just an act because he wants to bag me? If he is this perfect, why is he still a bachelor at his age?

Who am I trying to fool? Myself, that's who. I've not even attempted the poetry contest that I wanted to enter just last week, but now I am thinking about writing an entire book? I must be deranged. I do not have one speck of confidence in my ability to conquer such a quest. I am nothing more than a failed housewife. Beaten down and battered, without formal education, that has not written one iota of fiction in over ten years. Dreaming of publishing a book before even one attempt. It is the most ridiculous thing to even contemplate at this point in my life. Besides, what if Anthony found my book? Perhaps I am having bouts of mania brought on by stress. This is my life, not a whimsical novel I wish to write. Not a poem worthy of being commended nor a movie up for an Oscar.

Just

My

Normal

Housewife

Life.

And I hate it with every fiber of my existence to the very core of my being. At this moment, I hate my life more than I hate life, itself. What a feat: to hate my existence more than the filthy, putrid, searing hatred I feel right this very moment for the moon, the stars, and the very Earth that I spit upon. Blood-tinged saliva hides behind a set of perfect teeth, white as porcelain. My broken life secretly tucked behind an elaborate mirage of beautiful things. My mouth glares back at me from the mirror, teeth sparkling brightly almost in jest, lips twisted into a swollen sneer. It reminds me of every fake smile that has glided past me during my existence thus far. Every smile mocks my misery. Are their lives really enjoyable, or do most people fake it as I do?

Why have you stayed then? My mind begs me to consider this, but I've no logical answer in return. Why have I stayed when I've forgotten how to manage so much as the slightest genuine grin? I live in a world where every kiss placed upon my lips has been placed there by a narcissist. Beautiful teeth for a beautiful woman used to eat beautiful food in a beautiful house. This mouth is not for happiness. It is on reserve to echo agreements and nothing more.

Enjoy your pretend life, Sandra. Stay shut up in your beautiful house, to never partake in another delicious morsel of freedom again. I don't deserve it, all the wonders this life can hold. I obviously take every gift for granted, as I realize now that I've nothing really left. No job, no freedoms, no face even. I stare again at the grotesque woman in my mirror.

"Stay shut forever," my thoughts command my mouth, "until ribs are protruding like the starved Jewish ancestors of so many. Stay shut until your eyes follow suit. Stitch them up, dear mortician, to keep out the torturous dawn each waking day brings." How it is fleeting, my will to live.

I had another bad nightmare last night just like the one I had a while ago. This guy was throwing me around beating the shit out of me. I never saw his face, but it felt hella real. My date with Tee was so amazing, I'm disappointed my head fucked with me in this way. I was so relaxed and ready for a good night's sleep. I was hoping to have a steamy dream, honestly. I just can't figure out why I am having recurring thoughts of something so awful. I have never been in an abusive relationship. Actually, I'm kind of a bitch to guys sometimes. I definitely wouldn't put up with some shit like that.

Tiffany knows.

God help Sandra's husband if we ever meet. Homicide beckons me.

Tiffany unexpectedly dropped by earlier today and started ringing the doorbell like a madman. I yelled through the door that I was painting the house and couldn't open it.

"My hands, they're full of paint, Tiff. Can I give you a ring when I am through?"

She was not easily swayed and replied, "I know something's up, Sandra, and I'm NOT leaving until you let me in!" She sat down on my porch, and I knew I had no choice but to give in. I couldn't very well leave her out there all day, waiting for Anthony to come home and question why the hell there was a stranger participating in a one-person sit-in on our porch. Why would I even have company in the first place? Surely, he would wonder. No one has been to our residence in many years, particularly for my benefit. I slowly opened the door and bowed my head, trying to hide how battered I was but not really knowing how to accomplish the task. Tiffany had an absolute fit when I looked at her. She started ranting and raving about Tee being a lawyer and that there is a way out.

"There are people who will help you! Places you could go!" She begged for me to agree, and said we could leave immediately, but I simply cannot. No one has been able to help me all these years, and I will not risk anyone "helping" me now. I tried to explain my refusal. He would kill me if he found out I went behind his back.

"Maybe he will kill you, too!" I exclaimed at her. "Who knows what he is really capable of? The world is much too small, Tiffany, and maybe you haven't seen that reality yet. If this got back to him somehow – if Anthony found out, I just – I just couldn't live with myself if I put you in harm's way. You must promise me you will forget about this ridiculous plan of yours."

Her face fell in disbelief. "But it WON'T get back to him! How would it even? Tee could be very discreet until the perfect moment. This is complete bullshit, and you need to get away from this animal! He is such a great guy, so I bet he's a great lawyer, too. Just let him help you. Let us help you."

"No!" I repeated firmly. "And that is final. Please, Tiff," I begged her. "The legal community is much too small. You must believe me. My whole life is here in this house. There is nothing for me outside of these walls. Where would I go? Yes, I have funds I could access, but I cannot just walk away from everything and start new when I've no skills, no family, and nothing to even look forward to. It is my choice to stay in this relationship. Leave it be."

"Relationship?" She heatedly questioned me, pointing accusingly at my face. "Is THIS what you call a relationship? Give me a break!"

"Please," I whispered. "I am trusting you. Please, Tiffany, you are the only one I can rely on. If you let me down, I will truly have not one soul left to confide in."

Reluctantly, she agreed and left after a brief chat. I also requested she not drop by unannounced again. She nodded in agreement, but only after I promised to reach out on a daily basis to assure her of my safety and update her on the progress of my healing wounds. After my friend left, I realized what a burden had been lifted off of my shoulders. How thankful I am to have such a wonderful and loving confidant such as Tiffany in my life.

Finally. After almost a decade, I have someone I can speak openly with.

CHAPTER 7

I am beyond PISSED! My friend is getting the shit kicked out of her, and I can't do anything about it. This is complete and total bullshit. I knew something was going on but had no clue it was something this bad. I just didn't realize… and she looked so awful. And I am supposed to just sit around and watch helplessly until what? Until he kills her? Gah! I'm so frustrated!

Do you know the statistics on this kinda shit? Around 20% of violent crimes are committed by an intimate partner. Gun possession in a home with domestic violence present raises the chance of homicide by 500% or more! Does Anthony own a gun? I don't know! I'm feeling so lost, and all I have done since coming home from Sandra's is obsessively google about domestic violence. That was a terrible idea because now I'm even more scared for my friend than when I first saw her.

Another statistic: only 34% of victims injured by their partner end up receiving medical care. I'm POSITIVE Sandra's injuries needed to be addressed by a healthcare professional. The cut on her lip was being held together by a couple of butterfly band-aids, and her eye was such a deep shade of purple it looked black and is practically swollen shut. She definitely needed stitches, I'm sure of it. I tried to get her to go to the hospital but didn't bother asking her twice after her refusal.

Her house is impersonal as fuck, and she is locked up in it day in and day out like a motherfucking trapped animal. She didn't even look sad anymore. It was all fear

71

in her eyes. Or should I say "eye" since I couldn't really see one of them? If she is so scared, why won't she just accept my damn help? I don't get it! I guess I can't really understand something like this because I have never gone through it myself. She was so proud that I sold two paintings that, even in her misery, she kept apologizing for her absence at my gallery opening. I felt so guilty for being angry with her. She needs to check herself and her apologies at the door. I'm absolutely heartbroken for her and don't want her to have any extra stress on my account.

"Seriously, stop apologizing, and give me a hug," I said to her, softly. She folded into my arms like a frightened and innocent child. I don't know what else to do for her.

Having Tiffany around has made me realize that there is someone in my life that cares about me. Her visit gave me enough confidence to start my novel. Ah, my moods change so suddenly. This foreign, lighthearted feeling was suddenly squashed when Anthony graced me with his presence. I feel it's almost a talent of his: the entire environment changes – the very air seems heavier – when he enters a room. It's unbelievable how crushing his spirit is.

"What are you doing," he nods at my project and continues, "writing in that stupid journal again? Did you purge all of your big girl feelings, honey? Are you all fixed from your pretend therapy session? Hopefully, you'll be a better cook now that you've unloaded all of your superficial pain about being a wealthy housewife." He rolled his eyes before retreating, still mumbling audibly about how disappointing I am as a spouse.

I looked at the floor and whispered, "Actually, I'm writing a novel." Why am I still moved to answer him? *I am so weak*, I think to myself, as I awkwardly clear my throat.

"Pathetic." That was all he said before dissolving into a fit of laughter and heading to the bedroom. He's right, I am pathetic. "Miserably inadequate," as the dictionary puts it. He was out the door as swiftly as he had arrived, retreating after taking a quick shower. *Enjoy the bar, darling.*

I called Tiffany to see if she could cover my bruises with makeup.

I seriously feel so bad talking about my perfect relationship when everyone else's seems to be crumbling around me. When I got to work today, Claire practically demanded to know why I was unreachable all weekend. Last night, she had an awful fight with Carl, and he left. Today she doesn't seem that sad about it, honestly. She's livid.

"I needed you to come over and get fucked up with me! Instead, I put the baby to bed and watched The Notebook and drunk-cried alone like a little bitch!"

"So sorry, my supreme queen, I was out with Sandra last night. Her prob – I mean – it was just a busy weekend in between the gallery and stuff. I'm so sorry I let you down. I promise to make it up to you. Tell me everything, and let's make plans ASAP!" I stopped myself from spilling the beans about Sandra, but that was a close one. I heard the little voice in my head hastily remind me how small the world can be. It helped me remember my promise to keep quiet about someone's business that isn't mine to share.

Last night, I brought cake makeup over to Sandra's house to help teach her how to look presentable in public. Makeup absolutely works miracles. We had a couple of martinis before leaving the house and then hit every dim-lit bar that crossed our path, which happened to be four of them. I am so totally and ridiculously hungover, it should be a crime.

When I stumbled through the door intoxicated early this morning and saw my husband sitting in his chair, I knew he was waiting for me. He taught me a valuable lesson this morning: It doesn't hurt nearly as much when I'm two sheets to the wind. Not even in the beginning.

I got bounced off of more walls than I recall having in our house. After so many blows to the head, I just stayed there on the floor for a long time. Whether I was unconscious from the copious amounts liquor or the abuse, I'm not quite sure which it was. I woke up several hours later, partially underneath the dining room table, with a splitting headache. When I found my footing, I made my way to the mirror to assess today's damage. Seeing the fresh bruises across my neck, it jogged my foggy memory. After I lay on the floor, bleeding from my partially healed wounds (now gaping again), he wrapped his hands around my neck and squeezed. Oh, how I prayed for death at that moment. Just as my eyes began to droop, and I rejoiced over the everlasting freedom death's darkness was to provide me, he abruptly stood up and waltzed out of the room. I coughed and gasped weakly as I passed out, disappointed with his inability to follow through.

Avoiding Tiffany's calls isn't really working out. Every voicemail begins the same: "Sandra, I know you are there." But does she? *Am I really even here? What does that entail? Where is "here" anyway?*

When everyone around you has a dysfunctional relationship, it kinda makes you question your own. It feeds on all of your insecurities. That's what I did all day at work today. I looked around and saw all of the cheaters. I saw unhappiness and frustration. Bob and his perverted ways, obviously making up for something lacking in his marriage. I thought of Claire and Carl, failing and thriving and failing again, in a rollercoaster of a relationship. Even though they brought a precious daughter into this world that they both adore and would do anything for, it's just not enough to keep them together. Sandra and the horror story she is living in.

That just leaves me and Tee, and it makes me question why we would be the exception instead of the rule. Just when I was wondering why he hasn't called me since our perfect date, he called me right then. Maybe we *are* connected in some bigger kind of way. I guess it's possible we could end up having a great relationship even if everyone around me seems to be falling apart. He just feels too good to be true, but I definitely don't want to go through life thinking that way. I'm not trying to self-sabotage. We're going out tomorrow night again. Maybe it's time he stays over, so I can "properly evaluate" our situation. LOL

All the pessimistic feelings must be from the stressful emotions my friends are projecting onto me. I constantly feel guilty about the good things going on in my life. Who am I supposed to share everything with if I have this mental block? Damn, it's lonely at the top. I guess I can tell Claire about my life. She seems to be taking her breakup okay. She wants to go clubbing this weekend which is a good sign. Maybe Sandra would want to go. We had SO MUCH FUN last night when we went out! That woman is a fucking riot when she finally lets loose and relaxes. I'm feeling it today, though, holy hell. I wonder how she is holding up. She hasn't answered my calls, but she's probably sleeping off her hangover. I totally wish I could take a nap right now.

I finally decided to return Tiffany's calls, and she asked me around to her place for dinner and drinks. Reluctantly, I agreed. Fortunately, she left her costume makeup at my house. *I did a pretty good job*, I thought to myself as I surveyed my work. Tiffany, no doubt, surpasses me in the makeup department, but my face turned out just fine. I may even start going out and about after tonight. Tiff is so fluent in this fast-paced, fashionista world we live in today. Oftentimes, I feel so outdated and much older than my age.

My opinion of my makeup turned out to be less than reliable, so it seems. I was no sooner through her front door when she proclaimed loudly, "He did it again, that bastard!" All I could manage was a nod in agreement, as the tears began silently streaming down my makeup-covered cheeks. For the first time in many years, I allowed *all of myself* to let go. Every ounce of pain washed over and swallowed me. Guilt and shame lifted a bit, making me feel lighter; the tears cleansed my soul, in a way. I felt renewed after, even as my chest still heaved and shook with emotion.

The grief is immense for missing my mother, my deceased father, and the marriage I dreamt of. But, mostly, for myself. That person I thought I was to be. The woman I believed I was supposed to become. Like a struggling newborn, I've been labeled "failure to thrive" and have lived up to this lowly expectation of myself. I feel free somehow. Is this the result of one good, hearty cry? No, no. It's her. It has been so long since I've been enveloped with unconditional love, I've almost forgotten how to recognize it. Tiffany is a true friend; she calls herself my "ride or die" and reminds me of it often. And what have I given her in return? Constant worry and a secret to keep, even if it costs me my life. Ahhh, it is incredibly unfair to her. Although I do not believe life has to be fair, I have gifted her some peace of mind. I gave my consent for her to (when she is ready) talk to Tee about my dire situation.

"As long as I can remain anonymous for now?" I asked her, cautiously.

"Of course, of course!" She hugged me hard and repeatedly praised me for my courage.

Sandra is going to die at the hands of that asshole if I don't help her soon. She came over for dinner – which was surprising in the first place – and we ended up having a sobfest as an appetizer. She agreed to let me gab to Tee about her situation, but I cannot set up an appointment for her. YET. She will get there, eventually, and I hope it's sooner rather than later.

Holy shit! My perverted boss is giving Claire a hug, and he just slipped a light kiss onto her neck. She looks sooooo angry. What is it that? I smell something in the air *sniff sniff* but what is it? I can't quite put my finger on it... Ahhhhh *sniff sniff* that's it, right there... I smell a lawsuit! LOL! There seems to be a lot of that going around lately. I could give Tee massive amounts of business at the moment. Literally. So. Much. Drama.

I wanted tonight to be "the night" for us, but now with the Sandra stuff, I don't really feel like it's appropriate. She's so thick in my head that I can't imagine this being the right time to bring it to the next level with him. We're meeting at Caesar's at seven o'clock. I'll have to get there a little early to catch up with Tom.

I am missing that guy so much lately.

CHAPTER 8

I am now well into the second chapter of my novel, but I feel something is lacking. Whenever I do a quick read-through, I can tell it is good writing but something's *missing.* I cannot tap into that feeling – that spark – when a writer's passion speaks clearly through their work. When a story is so powerful and relatable that, when you read it, you are immediately transported to another place and time. I used to read my writing and wonder *did I really just write that?* Even though I know it to be fact. Unfortunately, it is just not there. At this point, I'm feeling like a complete and utter failure. This gift of writing was the only thing I felt 100% sure of. It is the only part of me I truly identify with. Without it (and upon the heels of everything else going on in my stupid, miserable life) why even go on? *Why bother?*

When I got to Caesar's at six o'clock, I realized I never told Tom that I made actual money selling my artwork. His eyes regarded me with a look of genuine excitement, and he praised me so hard. Tom is such a great guy, and I couldn't help but notice how good he looked tonight. No snide remarks, no laughter, and he seemed prideful when mentioning he was present the moment I discovered my love of art. *Mmmm, he sure is an eyeful, isn't he? I wonder if he thinks about me the same way.*

I have changed my goals back to realistic ones. I cannot expect to sit down and write a best seller while I am moping around in slippers all day. If I am going to continue to feed my inner demons, I am going to make sure it is done in a productive manner. I've decided to write a bit of poetry for the contest after all. It is socially acceptable to be long-winded and depressing in a poem but not an entire novel. I don't think anyone would get past the first chapter of the book I've started unless they were on some kind of self-destructive suicide mission.

With my recent episodes of mania, going from depression to motivation to downright madness, I do not think I'll be making any commitments to a long-term project at this time. I should stick with things that can be finished relatively quickly. Particularly, since I could very well die at any moment by my husband's hand. YAYYY to new projects!

On another note, I had assumed my recurring nightmare about death was based on my fears, but perhaps it is only my impending fate that I foresee. Dreams are a curious sort of adventure. I wish I could interpret them better.

Last night was great until I brought up Sandra. Don't get me wrong, Tee was super nice and understanding, but he told me there is nothing she can do but file a police report or attempt to secure a restraining order.

"But I know she won't do that," I whined. "She won't even let me tell you her name, so how am I supposed to get her to fill out official paperwork about this asshole?" He told me it's one of those "he said, she said" things. Best-case scenario, she documents everything. Takes pics of her wounds, jots down what happened during the incident, etc. If she won't pursue charges, no one can force her to.

"In our state," he explained, "it is not mandatory to press charges. She has a choice in the matter. We have mandatory reporters. If she, for example, went to the doctor to mention the abuse, that doctor would be required by law to file a report on her patient's behalf."

"But there's no way she will do that," I argued. "She didn't even go get stitches, and I'm sure she needed them."

"Sorry, Tiffany, you can't help someone that won't help themselves. Maybe she is happier than she leads on and just needed to vent." And that was that. I definitely wasn't feeling the magic after that convo, so we ended our evening with only a kiss. AGAIN. I think we're both frustrated at this point, but I'm still kinda glad we're taking it slow. It's such a nice change from the losers I usually go out with.

I have started on my poem, and I cannot tell if it is helping or harming the depression that's all but consuming me. For inspiration, all I have to do is gaze upon myself in the mirror. I am almost thankful I cannot yet see clearly through both eyes, for it is hard enough to accept my truth while looking out of one. If my injuries were less severe on my face, I know they would be worse in other places on my body. I also know, had that been the case, I would've continued working at the bookstore per usual. I imagine myself peacefully placing books on shelves and, to the surprise of my coworkers, spontaneously dropping dead right there in the aisle.

"Internal bleeding," they would conclude. It would be ruled a homicide. Or maybe a lesser charge of manslaughter, what with my husband's ability to manipulate others so easily. It would be shocking – a scandal, to say the least. Everyone in town would whisper, shaking their heads in disbelief. It would have neighbors questioning who else in their lives were falling victim to similar crimes. Who do we pass on a daily basis that is suffering in silence, bruised head to toe, and clothed in secrets?

The headline would read, "Prominent couple leads a violent double life. Husband charged."

I would prefer – if there was a preference scale to rank abusive wounds on – for all of them to be above the neck. You see, if injuries are above the neck and one wakes the following day, a concussion cannot necessarily be ruled out, but you're much less likely to have a severely impacted future from brain damage. The extent of the damage is pretty clear at that point, and there would be definitive outward signs of major physiological changes from a head wound. I feel you'd never *really* know if you had internal bleeding until it's just too late. But is that correct? I'm not sure. Maybe I'll never know, maybe I will. No matter, anyhow. My wounds cut much deeper than anything I've spoken of. Externally, they are mere scratches in comparison to the damage that's on the inside. My spirit is broken, and my mind is on an irreversible, never-ending rollercoaster headed straight for insanity. Choo-choo, full steam ahead!

Oh, how I despise him. Hate him. Wish he were dead even. If I did not hold such strong morals against murder, I'd entertain killing him myself. Yes, I certainly would. I'll just sit and relish in that sweet little thought for a moment longer. Maybe I was wrong; perhaps I still hold some dreams deep in my heart. I pondered this sweet scenario for a bit longer than I had anticipated.

I think Claire is really thinking about bringing a lawsuit up against Bob the perv. If he knew that she was considering it, I wonder if he would stop harassing us. Could he even control himself if he tried? He's probably so out of control because no one has *ever* done anything about it. It seems like it's second nature to him. Sexual harassment to Bob is like breathing to humans. One day, that perv is gonna pay. He'll get exactly the karma he deserves. All bad people do. Eventually. If not in this life, at least in the next.

I can only imagine pervy Bob and his sister, fat Becky, amidst all the demons in Hell. Ha! Should this be so funny to me? Claire and I entertained this topic of conversation for way too long. Sure, it sounds evil, but thinking of all the ways Bob could be tortured was way too amusing to stop. He has put Claire and I through hell, so it's really fitting as a pastime. Having him as a boss must be our karmic punishment for something.

I was glad to see Claire smiling again. After the liquor wears off, she gets really upset when Carl is gone. She is working with creeps all day and then consumed with being a single mom in the evening. Taking care of a house and Ciera all by herself, she has gone through more stress than someone our age should have to deal with. She acts like it doesn't bother her to have so much on her plate, but I know it's just a front sometimes. She is so strong, so determined, but she's not the same person when Carl is gone. They are so on-again, off-again but an otherwise amazing couple. Maybe after some growing up, they will be able to work it out. They were so young, I think sixteen, when they met. They got pregnant after a couple of years together, but that is still super young to be raising a child. They missed out on a lot of experiences other teens got to have as they transition to adulthood as parents.

And then there's me. I'm 23 and beyond ready to settle down, but I love the club, too. Decisions, decisions. Ugh! That's why I'm so strung out on Tee. He's older, isn't into the club scene, established in his career and adulthood. He doesn't live to drink and fuck, fuck, fuck like most of the guys I know. I'm sure since he doesn't have kids and has never been married, he might be ready to commit on that level, whereas guys my age aren't into that idea AT ALL. Obviously, we haven't talked about that yet since we haven't even been intimate. The sex and the settling down, I want it all. I want the sex part sooner rather than later. I'm getting impatient.

I spoke with Tiffany today, and she suggested I take photographs of my injuries. I am contemplating it but not positive I'm entirely comfortable with the idea. Having hard evidence of this sort of thing in our well-to-do society in high-class suburbia incites a twinge of fear in me. Things are so easily twisted. Revictimization and bullying are very real problems if my evidence should find its way into the wrong hands. Corruption is no stranger amongst the rich and powerful, I assure you. And what if Anthony happened upon them? God knows how he would react.

She also advised I document everything. I told her I already do, without specifically mentioning my habit of obsessive journaling. I do not provide specific dates in all of them, but I write in my notebook daily and have the year printed on the inside cover of each, always beginning on New Year's Day. The dates would be very easy to decipher and contain quite specific information in each one. New Year's Day. A day signifying new beginnings, renewed strength, and hope for a brighter future. It is a pretty accurate account of my entire life, considering the amount of writing I do. What else is there to fill my days anyhow? I don't see it doing any good or being helpful in any way. No one reads these;

no one ever has. My mother, sister, and husband are the only ones who even know I journal. That is all, and I don't even speak to two of those individuals. Technically, one could argue, I don't speak to any of them.

If only I could be as committed to my novel as I am to journaling. It would be such an enormous weight off of my shoulders if I had a larger outlet to express myself but the ability to remain secretive about my personal struggles. With fiction, that is achievable. How many novels start with a disclosure that everything is made up? Every last one. You've seen it over and over: "Names, characters, business, events, and incidents are the products of the author's imagination. Any resemblance to actual persons, blah, blah, blah…"

In a perfect world, my "fictional" tale would provide me with an independent, steady revenue to buy my way out of this soap opera life. I could divorce Anthony and live as an example to other women in my position. Help them somehow, if even only providing a reprieve from their day-to-day troubles. A bit of solace in the dark days of whatever struggles they're facing. Build them up, give them confidence. Show them independence is not only possible, but it is *waiting for them.*

How stupid of me, though. It is plain to see I cannot write these stories of inspiration. How would I compel others to strive for their independence when that very strength is lacking in me? I couldn't even tell my dear friend the truth when she asked how long domestic violence has been part of my marriage.

"Recent. Very recent," I lied. How was I supposed to reply? "10 years, 2 months, 17 days, and – would you like to note the time? It was on a Sunday." Much like the birth of a child, the date my marriage died will never escape my memory. I went on, further deepening the depth of my deception, "It's not all the time." I whispered, "Quite infrequent, actually. Just when I anger him."

"Even ONCE is too often, Sandra!" she raised her voice a bit, and it startled me. When she saw me flinch, she started to tear up. "Look what he's done to you, my friend. Look what he's already done to you. If you can't find the courage to fight him legally, the only way to save yourself is to fight him physically. Because what are you going to do if this goes on for years? Do you REALLY think you could survive for years like this? No offense, but you're a fucking mess, and it hasn't even been going on that long. I'm really worried about your safety if you don't recognize you deserve better than this." I looked at her in disbelief because she didn't understand my point of view at all. But how could she? It is so simple for her; it is black and white.

I nodded solemnly because she was right. As I retreated into my mind, I pictured the look on my husband's face as his dinner sailed towards him, not all that long ago, and I whispered, " It would only serve to anger him further, Tiffany. I know you're trying to help me, but –" my voice trailed and she cut me off, mid-sentence.

"No, what I'm TRYING to do is get you to save your own damn life!" Fantastic. Life advice from a 23-year-old. How have I gone so wrong that this is what it's come to?

such agony plagues
this wife of years
who spends
her nights alone
longing lost
leaving only despair
sanity no longer
is privy here
not being who she
could've become
loving 'til
heart's content
peace eludes
her price is paid
restless longing
and memories fade

darkness wins
but no one cares
beat again in
bitter nightmares
leave me, lover
oh, distant lover
you know me
not a speck
and shall
you seek
cherish your find
blame my source
the weakest mind

It's definitely rusty but will do for now. I'm feeling better already.
Poetic therapy never disappoints.

Tom wasn't working last night when I popped into
Caesar's, so I went again tonight to see if he was there.
Stalker much? I peeked into the bar first to make sure
Tee wasn't around, and the coast was clear. Not that I
didn't want to see him because it's always nice to see his
handsome mug, but I want to chill alone right now.
Alone with Tom and every other customer here, that is.

"Hey stranger," he drawled smoothly with a relaxed
smile.

"What's up, Tommyboy? Looked for you last night. Sat
here all by my lonesome for an hour waiting for Tee and
looking like a loser."

"I was using up my vacation time. What's new in your
life these days?"

"I sold another one of my paintings!" I exclaimed. "That makes me practically a professional, right?"

"Keep it up, doll, and I'll agree when you're making a living at it." That's Tom for you: soooo optimistic. Not! But hmmmm… he called me "doll." I could almost swear he was looking at me in some type of way.

"And I could quit pervy Bob's company," I squealed in glee just thinking the thought. And back to that other thought that makes me want to scream: HE CALLED ME DOLL.

What does that mean? He has never said anything like that before. Those eyes of his make me want to hop over this bar and onto his face. Now that's the kind of "happy hour" I'm in the mood for. I wish he would ask me out already if that's what he wants. But then there's Tee, and they know each other, too. It makes things more complicated, but I'm really attracted to Tom.

Guys are so confusing. Why do they only start hitting on you when you have something good going with someone else? I'm glad Tee wasn't at the bar because I was feeling all kinds of thick chemistry in the air. Plus, he and I aren't ready for a random run-in yet. I mean, what if I saw him out with someone else, or he witnessed the way Tom was clearly eying me up and down tonight. Now, back to Tom. I wonder if this flirting will go anywhere.

Anthony left for work, and the Nikon is on its stand waiting for the timer to be set. I'm so nervous and torn about whether or not I should even be doing this. If I follow through, I can put them on a flash drive. Maybe I will need to get a safety deposit box or somewhere to securely store it. If I ever entertain the idea of a police report, I don't think I will be hanging around the house gathering my items. I'm not too sure where I would keep something of this magnitude. I doubt I would ever go through with a report, but I know it's better to be safe than sorry. At least, I'm starting to.

.

I painted a new set of pictures over the last few days. They are mostly dark images. I finally broke down and bought the color brown. Lame. Probably because life is so fucking shitty right now. I have been really depressed about Sandra, and it's starting to distract me. Getting attention from two guys would normally be awesome, but that just stresses me out, too. Tee didn't give me very much hope about Sandra, and Tom didn't give me much hope about Tee. Everything is upside down right now, and I'm so sick of it.

Sandra didn't sound like she would even consider doing the bare minimum to build a case against her douchebag husband. I doubt she will do anything at all to help herself. I wish I could get her to see my point of view. If I were her, I would do everything in my power to take that wife-beating motherfucker down. I don't even know him and want to screw his entire world up.

I went above and beyond today! The pictures are developed. I was able to just print them off directly from the camera wirelessly, so I didn't even have to download them onto the computer. I cannot risk Anthony finding them, and he is very much superior to me when it comes to the digital world. I'm not sure what kind of monitoring he has on our computers around the house, so I put them directly from the camera onto a flash drive titled "Utopia" and put it onto my keychain.

If there is one thing my husband isn't interested in, it's anything he deems related to my writing. He doesn't even glance at it because he fancies it as utter nonsense, the unrealistic rantings of a bored housewife. I need to bring these photos to a safety deposit immediately. It is amazing to me, what I look like. Is it because of the HD that my face looks so bad, or am I just coming to the realization that my husband *did* almost kill me recently?

Am I ever going to be able to return to my work at Binded? My leave can only extend so long before they start to question my absence. I cannot continue to live this way forever, and he has removed the only activity outside of this house that I truly enjoy. I am a prisoner who has not had a fair trial. A bird in a cage. No hope for escape.

I simply refuse to wallow in my own suffering any longer. I will not stand for a life where I'm constantly forced to sit, to submit. In this journal, I hold so many secrets. He cannot imagine they're not the fantastical dreams of a young girl. Of course, he doesn't realize the secrets they hold inside. I stopped sharing intimacies with him so long ago. He wouldn't dare bore himself by choking down my literature. There are so many hidden tales between these pages, and I've barely an adventure to my name. It does make me wonder what secrets my husband has kept throughout all these years.

Soon, I will know what he hides. That is a bet I would take.

CHAPTER 9

I'm going to hang out with Claire tonight. Carl came back home, but all she did was cancel her sitter and tell him he needed to stay with CeeCee.

"Fuck that!" She yelled over the phone on her way to my house. "He thinks he can come and go as he pleases and mess up the only plans I had this week? Oh, hell noooo!" I know she's secretly glad he's home, though.

We're going to hit the town. Caesar's first, of course. Then we're going to a club called "The Cheetah" that Claire said is lit. It has three floors, lots of money-loaded bachelors, and all the free drinks we want. Okay, okay. That's not really the club special so much as just a talent of ours. I'm the queen of getting free drinks. Actually, I'll get us to the front of the line and maybe even a free meal out of the night as well.

I assured her, "Mad skills, baby. No worries there, Claire bear." But we didn't really anticipate what would happen when we landed at Caesar's.

Oh. My. Lord. Help me. What have I gone and done? It is unimaginable, unfathomable. I, Sandra Buchanan, made an appointment with, spoke to, and *hired* a private detective to follow my husband. That's right! I am truly in disbelief about my very own actions. I don't know what's gotten into me. I am spiraling out of control, obsessed almost, by even a minuscule chance that I could get out from under my husband's reign someday.

The man who can help me achieve that is named Liam Hanson.

This morning when I woke, Anthony was nowhere to be found. What's new? He does whatever he pleases, whenever he chooses. And who even works on a Sunday? Some do, I suppose. But also on Friday evenings, Saturday, and sporadic random nights here and there? A little far-fetched, even for the busiest associates. Don't get me wrong, I prefer it when my husband is out of the house. Admittedly, I have become increasingly curious about what he does with all of those precious hours of freedom he's afforded. No one to question him, nor to make him accountable for his choices.

On a whim, I contacted Mr. Hanson and inquired about his services. He suggested a meeting and, before I knew it, I was sitting across the table at a trendy coffeehouse with a man about five years my junior. I tried to focus on the task at hand and converse with him but, I have to admit, it was hard at times. Sandy blond hair and those puppy dog eyes. Is his name Hanson or Handsome? Perhaps I should've hired a woman. I'm feeling quite distracted being in the company of a man.

The conversation, once I reeled my thoughts back in, inevitably turned to my disheveled appearance and Mr. Hanson – I mean, Liam – asked if I sought medical care. Are there medical records to request? I sheepishly admitted I've never received any real, professional counsel at all: not medical, legal, nor any other kind available. He looked so sad for me. That look, I despise it. Pity. I quickly told him that I'd taken pictures of my bruises just recently, and his disposition brightened up a bit. I didn't mention it was just this weekend. Making all kinds of huge decisions at once makes me feel unstable and irrational after being dormant for so long. How would that look to this logical man? I'm honestly not sure I know how I look to myself, so I cannot really theorize how this stranger would see me.

"I placed them in a safety deposit," I told him. After his necessary retainer and all of our formalities were through, I turned over my information along with his fee. My parents left me a trust long ago, and I haven't had much need for it through the years. Money is nothing to Anthony, so he never cared to really control me in that way. He is very regimented in many aspects, but I can live a lavish lifestyle, should I choose to do so.

"I've moved my journals out of the house as well," I continued. I hold only the current year's journal in my possession at this time, and he requested a copy. It made me feel embarrassed and uncomfortable to think he would have a copy of my innermost thoughts.

"Put the copy in your deposit box with the others. I want to make sure everything is as current and up-to-date as possible." His eyes held such kindness in their depths as he praised the bravery of my actions. I looked away as I blushed. I'm so relieved he'll not have this journal in his hands. How mortifying would that be?

When we arrived at Caesar's earlier tonight, Tom's shift was just ending. He was dressed nice – real nice – in an ass-hugging pair of Levi's and a blue button-down shirt. It made his eyes pale to the lightest shade of ice blue that I've ever seen.

"Holy shit. How intoxicating is he?" I breathed in Claire's ear. "Holy wow! Is it hot in here?" I suddenly feel like I'm sweating out of nowhere.

"Mmmm... yummy! You have to go for that, girl. I won't even let you ignore this one. Invite his fine ass out with us tonight. You're long overdue for a piece of ass, yeah?" We were cracking up as we walked to the bar to greet my crush.

One of your crushes, I reminded myself. I glanced around

quickly to make sure Tee wasn't at the bar. It's a little disappointing I met him at Caesar's because... BECAUSE OF THIS EXACT REASON!

"Heyyyy, Tom! Want to join us tonight? It's on you!" I winked and laughed.

He was cheesing so hard as he came over to greet us. We all chatted for a bit and when Claire went to the bathroom, Tom focused those piercing blue eyes on me and took my hand. He looked at me so intensely, I felt like he could see straight into my soul.

Is he going to kiss me? My breath caught in my throat as he leaned in close and said quietly, "The night's on me if we can call it a date."

I blushed as I replied, "It sure sounds like I'm getting the better end of the deal."

"I'm going to close out. Be right back." He let go of me just as Claire returned.

She quickly commanded me, "Spill it!"

"Omerrrgooodddddd, Claire!" It was all I could manage. I was bright red and trying not to erupt in a fit of girlish giggles with my friend. We both ogled him as he grabbed his tips and said goodbye to his regulars, that laid-back smile probably melting everyone in its path.

As we were walking out, I thought I spotted Tee sitting at a table with a leggy blonde, Marilyn Monroe type, and I silently thanked the Universe we never made anything official. I don't think he saw me as I slipped out the door with Tom following closely behind, but I couldn't tell for sure if we flew under his radar. I quickly squashed those thoughts. I just want to focus on Claire being happy and carefree again, Tom being my *date*, and all of us having a great time at a hot new club. Date or no date, I'm still getting us to the front of that line. I don't like waiting.

By nature, I am somewhat of a nervous person. The first time I saw Anthony after my meeting with Liam, I was terrified. I kept wondering if my husband knew what I had done even though it was completely unfathomable. Anthony would definitely punish me if he knew. Mr. Hanson assured me he would keep very close tabs on him, so I shouldn't worry myself about him finding out at all. Nevertheless, that's where my thoughts took me.

My husband avoids my writing like the Plague, so he won't find out from my journaling. I could plot to have him murdered in these pages, leave it in plain sight, and he'd look right through it at his beloved drink. Even if the pages were filled only with:

DIE

DIE

DIE

DIE

DIE

Over and over, one upon another, it still wouldn't make a difference to him. In fact, he rarely notices anything about me at all unless I am in his way or, heaven forbid, an obstacle between him and his precious Jack. We live completely separate lives when he's not tossing me around or demanding I serve him. Or the occasional raping. Completely separate lives aside from those, though. Just our normal routine.

I've been asking myself all day if going out with Tom was a good idea. It was fun at the time, sure. But now I'm really doubting my decision. I have two men I am dating, they know each other, and I'm not very confident this is going to turn out very well. I think of all the drama at my office, and it makes me want to run far, far away from this whole situation.

Okay. I can figure this out. On one hand, Tee is uber-sophisticated and has all the qualities a woman would expect a man like him to have. He is self-assured, established, has loads of money, and he's a great kisser. That matters! A lot, actually. He seems to have a rational head on his shoulders, which is a great thing, but also he doesn't seem like the most exciting man. On the other hand, Tom has a lot of redeeming qualities also. He is my age, makes me belly laugh with his outlandish wit, he's charming, and scored major points when we were out with Claire. She really liked him, and that is so important. Spice Girls know what's up. *If you wanna be my lover, you gotta get with my friends.* Big facts.

But Tom has this air around him that I'm so drawn to. It's almost inexplicable. He's like a really strong magnet. Okay, focus. You have to figure this out. They are both good looking. They both have oodles of charisma, although they're on super different vibes. I hope neither of them brings up relationship talk because I have no idea what I would say. I can't choose right now. I'm way too conflicted. I'll just date both of them for a little bit. People do this sort of thing all the time. It does give me a little nagging feeling in the pit of my stomach, but I'm sure it will work out in the end. Just another date or two with each of them, and I'm sure I'll be able to make a decision before anyone gets hurt. Before anyone even realizes what's going on, I will break it off with one of them. But how do I keep Tom from knowing I'm still seeing Tee since he was there when we met?

It has been three days since I hired Liam, and I have had exactly three conversations with him since. Today, we will meet face-to-face because he has some photographs he wants to go over with me. Already. There is already evidence after only three days. I am in disbelief.

I decided to dress up a bit because I feel myself longing for this man's approval. It is in such bad taste to want to look good for this stranger, but divulging this incredibly *embarrassing* information about my marriage has made me feel like I have something to prove to him. *To seem successful in even the smallest way.* On the phone, we try to keep it strictly business, but our conversation has already taken a casual turn more than once. He puts me at ease about my situation and, ultimately, with myself. I suggested we meet at Caesar's but he refused. I was secretly hoping to go somewhere I've been before. Somewhere new just adds another layer of nervousness to my already tense demeanor. Liam said it would be best if we met at "Chic" which is the trendy coffee joint from the other day. Ahhh, good. It will still be a familiar territory.

I had provided him with pictures of my husband, important business addresses, license plate, make and model of his Jaguar, and all of his personal identification numbers like driver's license and social security. There was not much more I could do besides provide basic facts. I know very little about my husband's life outside of our house. I'm not sure who he still has contact with or where he likes to spend his time. Most of our friends stopped socializing with us years ago because of Anthony's unpredictable nature. Some people see him for exactly what he is. I took a few deep breaths in order to steady myself and calm my overactive nerves. Liam told me he had proof of something that my husband is doing behind my back. Am I really ready for this? My God, it's been only three days!

I spoke with Tiff earlier today, and she excitedly recapped her date with Tom. It sounded like it was getting pretty hot and heavy toward the end of the night. She made it crystal clear she was still interested in her lawyer guy, but I don't think it's a good idea to date them both. My stomach lurched. *It's just butterflies, calm down!* Am I nervous about this new information to be revealed, or is it Liam himself that has me feeling all tangled up? I'd be a fool to convince myself it wasn't the latter. I definitely should have hired a woman. I mentally scolded myself again and straightened my posture in an attempt to feign a level of confidence I don't actually possess.

CHAPTER 10

Sandra called me completely hysterical. "He treats her right, I bet! She has got to be a tramp, and I am not even sorry for saying that! Thinking she can sleep her way to the top, I'll bet. She has only made it to the top of my husband! I will bring them both down."

"Wait, slow down," I exclaimed. "What are you talking about, hon?" I had no idea what she was babbling on and on about.

"Anthony," she sobbed. "I hired a private investigator, and he took pictures of him out with another woman. Let me be completely honest for a moment. I do not – I repeat – *do not* care if he is sleeping with someone else. I just cannot believe he takes her out. I have been stuck in this godforsaken house for years, and now he is out gallivanting around town with someone on his arm. No doubt, he's wining and dining her, as if he's going to provide her with some kind of security someday. Give me a break! Well, I'm going to make sure that doesn't happen. Tramp or not, angry or not, I have to help this woman so she doesn't end up in the same hell that I've landed myself in. He cannot do this to someone else."

"Anthony is cheating on you?" I was shocked. This man is un-fucking-believable.

"Yes," she answered quietly. "I cannot mind it too much, really. It keeps him occupied and away from me. But why does he do this, Tiffany? He is obviously capable of treating someone with respect. I don't understand. Why is he so mean to me? What did I do?"

"You can't understand crazy," I assured her.

She cried, "What's wrong with me that makes him act that way?"

"Stop blaming yourself," I commanded her. "That's ridiculous. None of this is your fault. We need to talk about what you're going to do. What's next?"

"I really haven't a clue what I'm supposed to do," she admitted.

Truthfully, I feel no real jealousy for this woman running around with Anthony. If we had a beautiful picture-perfect relationship and I was faced with this surprising news, it would be devastating. I imagine it is tremendously painful for spouses that believe their marriage is whole and concrete when they find out about the infidelity. It likely feels confusing to them, and they cannot fully understand the reason why their partner would bed another. The shock and horror, the immense pain felt by the entire family, would be traumatic. Not I. Anthony does this for one reason and one reason only. It's what drives him in every aspect of life. Narcissistic and manipulative, he is one hell of a selfish human being. This other woman has *no idea* what kind of controlling swine she is dealing with.

I pity her. I fear for her. She is, obviously, caught up in the maddening twist of deception Anthony is so adept at weaving. The devastation she will feel when it's revealed that her "great catch" is a married man just sickens me. She could be a victim as much as I am. It saddens me that another individual is being affected by my broken marriage.

I'm still sleeping like shit lately, and I'm totally over it. Nightmares every night, and the same ones repeating themselves. It is literally causing anxiety that is preventing me from falling to sleep in a decent amount of time, and then I'm a complete bitch all morning. When did my life become so stressful that it's turned me into an insomniac? Ohhhh yeahhhh. It's when I found out my friend was getting the shit kicked out of her, and I decided to start dating two men.

Also, it's Tom. Tom is so amazing. We've been talking a lot, and his call woke me up last night right after I fell asleep. I chatted with him for a few minutes, but then I was restless all night after that. Having a social life is really hurting my beauty sleep. If I was getting laid by either of these fine men, I wouldn't mind as much about my lack of sleep. At least if I was getting a piece of ass, maybe I wouldn't be a bitch all day. So, wait. Why am I not sleeping with either of them? It seems like a pretty appealing idea.

I had a dream last night that was terribly bothersome. It was about Tiffany. Someone was hurting her. I'm sure t's because I went on an awful tantrum to her about my broken marriage, and my husband didn't come home last night. *Again.* I'm sure I am projecting. I am so anxious about Tiffany, myself, this mystery woman running around with my husband, and life in general.

In this particular dream sequence from last night, Anthony was throwing Tiffany around like a ragdoll – not at all unlike my personal situation. It hurt my heart so deeply that I was unable to save her from him. I understand what's happening. I feel such guilt over Tiffany's concern for my safety. I also feel scared for this mystery woman my husband is cavorting around town with. I am simply plagued with so much inner turmoil that it's spilling over into my dreams.

I started thinking about her, this mystery woman. The thought of her is so foreign to me that I cannot even fashion her face from my memory alone. It was so brief, the glimpse I had of her photograph. Although it was just yesterday, I cannot for the life of me picture her now. *I could retrieve the file and thumb through the photos a bit.*

I went to the closet to get the large envelope Liam had given me. Turning it over in my hands, I reconsidered and tucked it back away under the floorboard. My safe spot. As safe as anything *can be* in this house, that is. As I stashed my treasure away, I wonder again why I'm not more upset over my husband's affair. Surely, I should be jealous, angry, hurt, or feel... *something*. Anything other than panic for this woman, a stranger sleeping with my husband, who may or may not know I exist. This has to be unnatural. I must be weird.

Our love has been gone for such an incredibly long time – or was it ever even there in the first place? For years, I didn't want to see that it had all but disappeared, and the chance for reconnection transitioned from slim to none. I actually no longer want Anthony on any level. I don't long for him physically, spiritually, not as a best friend, confidant, or other. I will always remember the person he was, but I will never forget the monster he became.

I had an awesome date with Tee last night, but I didn't really want to tell Sandra about it. I hate that I'm censoring myself around my friends lately, but she was ranting on and on about her husband cheating, and I didn't think she would appreciate my story about room service, champagne, strawberries, and the most amazing, handsome as fuck man on the planet.

Last night, I seriously felt like Julia Roberts in Pretty Woman, sans the whole prostitute aspect. I'm not actually a whore, and we definitely kissed on the lips. A lot! He took me to the Crowne Hotel downtown, and I was treated like royalty all night. I still didn't give up a piece of ass, but he didn't pressure me at all. Seriously, what is my problem at this point? I wanted to, but I couldn't. I kept thinking about Tom, and I'm like GET OUT OF MY BRAIN! But my head wouldn't stop messing with me, and I couldn't just fuck Tee while I'm thinking about Tom, so I lied and said I was on my period.

Tee never mentioned seeing me out with him, so I guess he didn't. That's definitely a good thing. A girl could get used to being pampered like this, but a few more nights of the royal treatment, and I won't have an excuse not to sleep with him. Claire said she would've already done it. But, really, who wouldn't by now?

"Think about it, though," I argued. "How long does the princess treatment really last after you put out, Claire?" I'm just not trying to give it up that easy. A few nice nights are great, but I'm down for the long game. No free milk from this cow, guys! Hey, did I just compare myself to a cow? Speaking of cows, dinner at Claire and Carl's place tonight was off the chain! Seconds of everything and stuffed to the max. I literally feel like a cow. Claire's man really knows his way around a kitchen. She is so lucky he doesn't think cooking is solely a woman's work.

When I finally walked in the door from work, since I went straight to Claire's after the office, I quickly plugged in my iPhone. I hate when I'm out and it dies. I cannot constantly keep dropping fifteen bucks on crappy charges. It's so frustrating. When it powered up, I saw I had a voicemail from Tom. I guess my making out skills are on point! I hope I'm on his mind as much as he's been on mine. After Tom's voicemail, there was an unfamiliar number. It was news soooo good that I almost peed my pants, seriously.

"Tiffany, hi! This is Mary Sue Becham from Creative Perspective Art Gallery. Ray, from Binded Books, gave me a ring and said I should check out some of your work. I'd like to set up an appointment at your availability. We may be interested in a collaboration and are currently scheduling individual artists a couple of months out. There are a few photojournalists that I have on the calendar to interview local artists I've featured, and they may want to include a few of your pieces. Please give me a ring at your convenience or, if it's better, we can hash out the details via email." She included her contact info, but I didn't even wait before disconnecting the line.

Oh. My. God. Oh. Em. Gee. Oh my God. Oh. MyGodohmyGod OHMYGOD!!! I can't fucking believe this. I have to tell Sandra ASAP what her freaking boss did for me. Unbelievable. But oh geez, this is even more good news for me, and she has so many problems she's dealing with right now. Would it pep her up or make her feel worse? Maybe I'll just wait and see how Mary Sue feels about my paintings and then tell Sandra. If she doesn't like them, there is really nothing to tell. I can't wait!

I vaguely recall Anthony slipping into bed a little after sunrise this morning, but when I awoke at 9:00 o'clock, he was gone again. Had I been more awake at the time, I would've paid more attention to see if there was a lingering scent of perfume or smudge of lipstick present. I'm only slightly curious. What selection of perfume does she dab behind her ears before my husband nibbles at them? And how would Anthony react if I suddenly purchased the same brand? I can only imagine his facial expression as he catches his first whiff of the familiar scent. Just toying with some fun ideas. He has been playing mind games with me for a decade. If he likes games so much, it would only be right for me to return the favor. It's healthy for married couples to bond over shared interests, right?

Claire wants me to stay with her for a couple of weekends coming up soon. Carl is going fishing and then hunting with the guys, and she doesn't feel comfortable staying in the city alone with Ciera. More importantly, though, she does not want to go fishing or hunting.

I called Mr. Hanson to see if he had information – actual concrete information – on the woman in the file he had provided. He told me he was just getting around to calling me, and we could meet at Insomnia, a coffeehouse a few miles from my home. He saw Anthony with *another woman* as well as the first, and he didn't want to give me any particulars because he was still working out a few details he was unsure of.

I raised my voice in protest, "I don't want this other woman – or *women* – to be victimized, Liam!"

"I hear you and understand your concerns, Sandra, but I have to figure out exactly the situation we have here before you can take any action. We can't just jump to conclusions, or people *will be* hurt." He emphasized those two words, and they echoed in my ears long after the call ended. What is he not telling me?

When I arrived an hour later, I sat at the table and demanded, "Why did you want to meet if you're withholding information from me?"

"Because I wanted to make sure you're okay. How are you holding up? How are you handling all this? You look fantastic, San. I mean, your injuries are healing up very nicely. Good, good." He straightened up a little and cleared his throat. It was only later that I realized he seemed flustered as he spoke.

"I am finally taking control of my life for the first time in years, but I'm feeling kind of impatient if I can be completely honest."

His smile grew and spread into his eyes, "You can always be honest with me."

"I'm having horrid nightmares every night," I confided in him.

"It's fitting to meet at Insomnia then," he joked, and we laughed about the name of the place he had chosen. "What are they about? Have you tried meditating before going to bed? Or melatonin? Chamomile tea?"

"Lately, most of them involve my good friend, Tiffany. Maybe they would dissipate if I spoke with her about them, but I don't want to drag her further into my horrible world of paranoia, lies, and violence. I cannot burden her any more than I already do."

"Your world isn't filled with those things," he corrected me. "You are filled with love, undying hope, and expanding your mind to uncover your truths. Truths that are setting you free. Anthony's world is filled with negativity, but your pure soul won't allow you to mirror his ugliness. You're like a beacon of light, Sandra. Don't discount all of the beauty your friendship brings to the table."

I could feel the heat rising to my face. "No," I shook my head. "She should be having the time of her life right now."

He searched my eyes, "But don't you see, Sandra? So should you."

CHAPTER 11

I met with Mary Sue, and it went okay. Meh. She pointed out a few paintings and said stuff like, "I really enjoy the depth in this." I guess she doesn't want to put any of them up in her gallery because she never said anything more about it. She kept talking about painting and geometry and a bunch of shit that I don't really understand. I don't get it. She said I have a lot of "potential" and I should pursue "formal" training. She gave me the number of a private art instructor she refers people to if she believes they could "be something significant."

Whatever, bi-atch. No, no. I'm not bitter at all. It just seems like a private art teacher is a little out of my fucking price range at the moment. I'm positive it's more than the perv will ever pay me, so why even bother checking into it? Speaking of the short, bald, fat pervert, Claire is seriously thinking about suing him! I totally have her back on this one. I would be so down to testify or witness or be in the damn suit. Whatever they do for this sort of thing, whatever the details, I'm totally on board. I told her I could ask Tee about what she should do, but I think he's going to start charging me for legal advice if I keep bringing up drama at every date.

Okay. I may have felt a tiny pang of jealousy over the affair. Or, is it plural? *Affairs.* After meeting with Liam yesterday (which was actually quite pleasant, given the circumstances) I started wondering why have I stayed faithful to a man like my husband? How did I let my marriage get this out of control? How can I still remain loyal to this evil man? Through countless lost relationships with family and friends, loyal. Dreams of being a writer long gone. I lost my virginity to this man and have remained steadfastly faithful. I can understand, to a certain extent, how a person can let a dysfunctional relationship rule their life for a spell of time. I cannot understand how I let this crumbled relationship rule my whole entire being? So much so that I've lost parts of myself along the way. What is even left of me?

I question if I've any thoughts that are really even my own. Political opinions, what are those? I vote straight Democrat, as Anthony instructed me long ago. I go through the motions of living, but I barely feel my own breath moving in and out of my lungs. I've been on autopilot up to this point. Tiffany's friendship has revived a certain part of me, and I feel awake for the first time. Still coughing, metaphorically, and unable to breathe fully on my own, but I am trying. I have never even once been truly independent in life. *But I think I want to.* It's such an invigorating idea! Sure, I remember how I felt in those moments before I transitioned from my parents' house to share Anthony's. It was exciting. I felt like I was gaining independence because I was leaving the family nest and growing up. Little did I know, I was only gaining a new master. For a few moments, before I knew what my future held, I felt like a real adult. Now, I'm afraid I'm no more than a grown child.

I haven't heard from Tee since we had our last romantic night at the hotel and, surprisingly, I haven't thought to get ahold of him, either. For the last three days, I have been too busy with Tom. He is the biggest sweetheart! He has been going hard trying to impress me, I think. Picnics in the park, flowers at work, and cute texts are filling my blissful days.

"Keep him!" Claire screamed at me. "Lock him up, throw

away the key, and never let another bitch near him ever, EVER again!" She has a point, though. I have been racking my brain searching him for flaws. Does he have any? He has a steady income. Owns his condo. Nice car. Nonsmoker. In school, and on his way to a brighter future. I just found that last one out. He's going to school for architecture. All of this AND PICNICS, one of the greatest things in the entire world. Basking in the sunshine surrounded by food is seriously the best date ever. Tee who? Just kidding!

I will admit, though, I'm a little cautious around someone who seems *too perfect*. Maybe I'm just being stupid, but I don't want to fall for someone and then find out everything was fake. I mean, Sandra thought her hubby was this great guy when they met – her knight in shining armor coming to sweep her off her feet – and he ended up being the devil incarnate. I guess you never know sometimes. They say Ted Bundy was really charismatic and handsome, too. Wow, talk about being wrong about someone's character. Not that I think Tom is a killer or anything crazy like that. Just saying, we only see what people allow us to see.

My eye is officially healed up, and my bruised ego will shortly follow. It really is amazing how much my mood improved once the physical reminders of the battery started to disappear. Lovely again, I suppose. *Am I lovely, though?* I question my reflection.

Maybe I should give up on Tee and focus my energy on

Tom. I mean, once you get past the so-called wit, he is very pleasant. He is a hearty, delicious piece of eye candy on top of it, too. Anyway, I think I'll call him after I sort through the mail. Sorting is my "me" time. My mind wanders and ponders while I update my lists, sort the bills, and recheck my budget. By the time I finish, I hope to know how I'll bring up the subject to my soon-to-be man. I don't want to freak him out if he feels like I'm rushing things.

After what seems like an eternity of quarantine, I can finally return to work. I am a tad nervous, as I would prefer not to field any questions from curious coworkers regarding my absence. As long as I am able to keep my emotions at bay while answering, I'm sure my first day back will be fine. I plan to work hard and keep to myself. That is typically my go-to approach anyway, but I will try to make a conscious effort. There are a few younger people that I chat with, but the turnover at Binded is appalling. I just pray no one tries to pry into my personal business.

I tried to call Sandra this morning, but she didn't – or wouldn't – answer. I hope she's okay. I really worry about her, especially when we lose contact for a few days. It would make me feel a lot better if she would just leave that loser husband of hers. How can someone like her stand to be knocked around? It's absolutely demeaning. If you ask me, he could use a good beating himself. Maybe it would teach him a lesson if someone knocked him around, but I doubt it. People like him are so fucked up in the head, he probably can't even tell right from wrong. Unless they are the ones being wronged, of course. Then, injustice is sooo obvious to a narcissist, and I'm sure they never let that shit go, punishing their perp relentlessly.

I have made it to lunchtime, and all is well within the four (figuratively speaking) walls of Binded Books. Walking into work was like being born again. The bright lights blazed overhead. The bustle of people all around. How magical and wonderous books are — teaching anything to anyone. No discrimination between the covers. No harsh words from the mass markets. And best yet, there were no questions from coworkers. Just multitudes of kind smiles and even kinder words. Walking back into my marvelous world of retail instantly brought me back to life.

I inhaled deeply .*I am home.*

When I walked – more like sleepwalked, I'm so tired – into work this morning, Claire bound up to me.

"What's got you so chipper?" I asked her, groggily.

"Make-up sex," she smiled brightly.

Apparently, Carl moved back in with Claire "for good" this time. This is practically becoming a monthly ritual with these two. Together. Apart. Together. Apart. And now, together... again. But I support my friend in her pursuit of happiness. Unconditionally and fully, I always support those around me without judgment.

Speaking of together, Tom dropped a little hint last night about being exclusive. I kinda played dumb and pretended like I didn't catch his drift. I hope he doesn't bring it up again. I had time to think, and I'm not sure I'm ready to cut ties with Tee. I thought that was what I wanted, but I'm constantly teetering back and forth. Tee called me today, so that's what changed things. We are going to lunch tomorrow. Casual dining, no big deal. I'm really having a good time taking it day by day. When I'm not stressing about choosing one of them, it is enjoyable having both of them. No reason to feel guilty over it.

It's not like I'm anyone's property or "spoken for" in any way. I'm so glad Tee asked me out for tomorrow and not tonight, though. I am beat! Tom has been keeping me up until ridiculous hours, and I just want to crash the fuck out tonight. I'm shooting for a solid 16 hours of slumber before work tomorrow. HA! If Tee asked me out for tonight, I don't think I could've said no. It is hard to say no to him, and I have a suspicion he's pretty used to getting his way.

I cannot believe I am doing this. I am sitting on the toilet writing in my journal because I'm so frightened. Anthony is staying in tonight and, so far, everything is fine. That is the truly maddening aspect of this. It has been an entirely pleasant evening. I've no complaints at all, really. He is not drinking tonight, and I actually find that incredibly unsettling. God, I am so broken. Why am I more comfortable if the alcoholic drinks? I am scared – no, terrified – and the little butterflies in my midsection are extra restless. They try to convince me everything is okay, yet flutter incessantly.

Anthony is the problem here, not you! Stop being a ball of nerves or he will catch on. He is incapable of change, he is cheating, and he is PRETENDING right now. I need to remember, during these hours of weakness, that my secrets are saving my life and securing my future. These rare, singular moments of peace have led me to stay through all of these painful years. I've compromised my own happiness to walk on eggshells in my own home.

I question God if Anthony has the ability to quit drinking. To treat me respectfully? But there is only silence in response. We danced around the living room like we were twenty again. I had forgotten how graceful he could be. I laughed; I feigned pleasantries. *Why is he doing this to me? Was it all a big misunderstanding? How does he cause me to constantly question my love for him, to contemplate my loyalty to him?* This, alone, is the reason I have stayed. I am not a housewife staying "for the kids." I am not here because I cannot make it in the world alone. I must remember I am *capable* even if I've never attempted it before. Sometimes I tell myself that I could not make it in the world, but I know deep down it's just an excuse.

I have a trust fund. I would be fine. My insecurity is just a tool that I use to hide from the truth. I stay because of that little bit of hope. The hope that one day, I will not have to worry if my husband is going to backhand me. That he will live up to the person I've incorrectly painted him as. The hope of living happily ever after and saying, "See? This is what all of the struggles were for. Lots of mistakes and many hard times, but just look at us now. Look at us now," I would repeat triumphantly. But after so many years, there is nothing redeemable here. Even if I were able to utter that phrase, I'd never have the ability to actually believe it myself. If Anthony were to make a complete 180 today, we are beyond repair at this point.

I am beyond repair. I smile sweetly at my husband as he spins me around the living room, and I put forth my best effort not to flinch as he dips me.

I am thinking about canceling my lunch date with Tee.

Last night, I had the same dream that I always have where I'm getting knocked around, but the difference this time is it was Tee doing the knocking. Now I feel all weird because I woke up super freaked out. I guess it's kinda messed up to cancel a date because of a nightmare, especially a recurring one that started before we even met. It felt so real and was so scary. I just have the creeps now. If my dream is anything close to what it feels like to be abused, I'm not sure how Sandra has stayed with her husband for so long.

I tried to fight back in my dream, but I couldn't get my body to cooperate. My arms were heavy and moving really slow. They weren't helping me in my fight at all. Maybe my subconscious is telling me I really do like Tom more, and I should give up and let go of Tee. It was just a *dream*, though, and Tom didn't ask me out to lunch. Tee did, and I'm hungry for some free food, babyyyy! Besides, it's not like anything bad will happen while we're out at a restaurant in the middle of the day. I can't let a little stress-induced nightmare keep me from landing my dream man. Everything will work out fine in the end. Eventually, I'll only be with one of them. I'll figure it out soon, I'm sure.

I need to control myself and my thoughts. My poor father, God rest his soul, has probably rolled over in his grave from all the years I've stayed with my unworthy husband. I can still hear him begging me not to return to him. It was only the second time he knew that Anthony had physically harmed me. It wasn't *really* the second time, though. I had already lost count by then. My father recalled a story to me that day. I remember it often, and I find it difficult to believe the fearless little girl he spoke of grew into the meek woman I have become.

"When you were a little girl, an older boy was pushing around your sister. You wouldn't stand for it. That boy, a year older than you, was lying on the sidewalk before he even knew what had hit him. You helped Suzie up, brushed off her knees — like the born nurturer you are — and walked her proudly home on your arm. Walk away, Sandra. Let us help you. Let all of us protect you, and you'll see that everything will be all right without him. I promise you," my father begged me. "We will brush off your knees, smooth out your skirt, and watch over you until you feel safe again. Do you remember that day, Sandra? Please, don't go back home to him. Not again. It will never change. Your marriage will always be this way, don't you see that?" I started crying, and he knew by the look of resolve in my eyes, my tears were only because I would choose to stay. "You are my little baby, Sandra. I don't want to outlive my child."

He always called me his baby. It was sort of a running joke, and it drove Sue crazy. Maybe that's why I left. To prove I wasn't the baby. I could make my own decisions, and I felt I could repair my broken relationship if I just *loved Anthony enough.* My father got his wish and did not outlive me, at least. It broke my mother's heart when I walked out of their house and back to my husband's. I let both of them down. I let everyone down. And where did such a steadfast devotion get me to? Life next to a man who has *never* shown an ounce of loyalty in return.

CHAPTER 12

It always bothered me when people would complain that someone was "too nice" to continue dating them. I had a friend, Melissa, in high school who broke up with this great guy who treated her like a queen. He pampered her, had a killer smile, and got along with all of our friends. Offhand, I can name three other girls who wanted him during the time he was doting over Melissa. I thought he was "the one" for her even though we were really too young for lifelong commitments. Their romance was short-lived, though, and I was shocked when she abruptly broke it off. When I questioned her, she confessed her only complaint was that he was "too nice." I went absolutely crazy!

"That's not a thing!" I ranted. That was literally the only acceptable guy I had seen her date up to our senior year in high school, and she was breaking it off why? WHY? I lowkey understand now. When I was friends with Tom, he had this dry and sarcastic sense of humor. He would jab at me all the time. Witty and pretty insulting, really, but hilarious. He still makes me laugh constantly, but his jokes are *different* since we started dating. They're safer. He's so freaking nice all the time that it automatically makes me suspicious of him. Is there something wrong with me? Is this a weird reaction?

It honestly has me overanalyzing everything and trying to find some sort of fault in him. Maybe he is a people-pleaser type, and that's okay. I just never really got that vibe from him before we started dating. What happened to the Tom I know and love? NO! Not "love" love. Not real love. I positively did NOT mean it like that at all. Friendly, platonic love. The insulting, pessimistic, bad-boy bartender appealed much more to my lustful side. Maybe Melissa was onto something. Being too nice can come off the wrong way.

Anthony and I made love last night. Consensual sex has become such a rarity in this household, as it's ruled by a raging alcoholic. It was a nice experience when I closed my eyes. It's not that I don't find my husband attractive because I do. He is a very good-looking specimen. But when someone scars your heart so many times – over and over, continuously and to no end – year after year, the painful memories stack higher and higher upon one another. It's becomes such a *task* to find them sexually stimulating anymore.

My mother once said, "Every stranger, young and old, rich or poor, has a right to your heart's generosity, should you deem them worthy. If they slow the beating – if that warm blood of yours starts running cold – turn away from them. Whatever you do, don't let that person ruin the gifts you hold inside of you. Think of the rest of the world. They'd miss out on so much of what makes you, you. So many others will cherish the love that one person took for granted." I closed my heart to Anthony long ago, so my blood still runs warm with love to give; yet, I have not completely turned away from him. Not fully, not yet. Why did I still feel a pang of emotion as we made love last night?

Why are you even referring to it as "making love" in the first place? Because, for once, it was consensual? Are you mad, woman? At first, I studied his face as he traced kisses along my neck. No doubt, he was thinking of another woman. I bit my tongue, suppressed my emotions, and enjoyed every sweaty moment after shutting my lids. But in those seconds, with my muscles quivering and my back arching in pure ecstasy, it took every bit of my resolve not to cry out another man's name as I reached orgasm. *Oh, that's never happened,* I shockingly thought.

Swiftly, my mind shut down and a peaceful sleep overtook me for the first time in months.

My lunch date with Tee was nice, but his mood seemed off somehow. He did ask me to go out with him tonight and when I said I had plans, something in his eyes flashed. Anger? Surprise? A cross between the two? I know he is not used to rejection, but I already made plans with Claire, so he'll just have to get over it. Right before I left for lunch, she asked if Tom and I would double with her and Carl tonight. She must've anticipated me making plans with Tee, and she slid into my schedule right under the wire. That girl knows what's up. Truthfully, I think she only wants to double to keep me spending more time with Tom and less with Tee. She plays favorites and doesn't even try to hide it. I have no clue what they have planned, but I'm stoked to hang with my bestie. I just hope my favorite couple doesn't bring drama tonight. I don't feel like being a referee for another end-of-the-world breakup.

But back to Tee's strangeness today. The lunch was okay. Normal convo and we were getting along fine. The food was delish, and we made plans for tomorrow evening. He always orders the right thing for me, and he takes us to all the best places in town. When he kissed me goodbye, it was super passionate. Like, weirdly passionate for being in public. I lost my breath a little when he pulled me tight toward him, and it was definitely out of left field after a pretty lowkey meal. When I got back to the office and recapped to Claire how he grabbed me tightly before our kiss, I winced a little because it hurt. Low and behold, I have two tiny thumbprint bruises below my ribcage. The kiss was great, don't get it twisted, but it freaked me out a little bit. So much for wearing a midriff tonight for our double date. Ugh.

He could tell I was lying. I don't lie often and when I do, I don't do it well. My whole marriage is a sham, I reminded myself while clinging to my justification. I need to channel that energy and make myself sound more believable than I think I am capable of. Whatever I *should have said* when I unexpectedly heard the front door open after lunch, I did not say.

Instead, I just blurted into the receiver, "I *said* you have the wrong number! Damn telemarketers," I complained loudly and stood up quickly from my comfortable position. How swiftly I transformed my appearance, from lounging in the recliner to rigidly staring into my husband's cold eyes. I could tell that he had a hunger stirring inside of him, and it definitely wasn't for me. But I didn't much care. For the second time in just over twelve hours, we explored each other as if our bodies were part of some unchartered territory we'd never before seen. His mind likely whisked him away to a realm filled with leggy blondes and fat lips. A place where perky-breasted women keep their mouths shut and their legs open, no doubt. Who am I to judge? I was in another dimension myself.

As the afternoon sun showed brightly through the living room window, I mentally escaped to a place with someone new. I do feel it's helping me to move on, in a way. I will grasp ahold of anything to make this upcoming transition possible. In between raspy breaths, how deeply I yearned for a new life. In my imagination, I've changed my husband in every single way possible. It was no longer him that I was making love to. After we finished, Anthony got up, dressed, and wordlessly waltzed out the door as quickly as he had appeared. Every time he leaves, I'm the happiest me that I am able to be. I rolled over, still lying naked on the floor, and hit redial.

"I apologize profusely that I hung up on you," I whispered breathlessly into the receiver.

"No worries. I understand completely," Liam replied.

Tom picked me up tonight, and we met Claire and Carl at the Wall. This bar has killer drink specials and no cover charge. We wanted to start out somewhere cheap so we didn't end up spending a hundred dollars in a few hours which is very easy to do. Claire and I drank free, and the guys split a bucket of beers. Carl and Tom get along great even though they are very different people. I was glad their conversation flowed so easily because maybe the four of us could start hanging out more often. Claire and Carl make such a cute couple. Carl with his light skin covered in tattoos and Claire with her dark skin and sweet, playful smile. Claire could probably turn any guy into the other half of a cute couple, though. She is just an all-around great person, inside and out. A little spunky underneath but (like Gizmo) harmless if she's fed on time. LOL

Seriously, though, Claire is the kind of person people just gravitate towards. Tom is that kind, too. He interacts well with people, putting them at ease as soon as they meet. He's a social butterfly, as they say, and can hold a conversation about anything from cars to sports to – well, he's actually kind of a man's man, now that I think about it. I was starting to freak because he kept on doing these ultra, over-the-top, perfect acts of romantic sweetness, and I was honestly questioning if he was nothing but a sensitive wuss underneath a hot bod. But when we went out dancing, it changed everything. Mr. "way too nice" Tom turned into "get your fucking hands off my girl before I beat your ass" Tom. That's right! We were all out on the dance floor and this creepy guy next to us started trying to move in and dance on me. Literally ON ME. I shrunk closer to my date, trying to shake him off, but he wouldn't take the hint. When he put his hand on my forearm, Tom stepped in between us and shoved him back a little.

"She's spoken for," he snarled, looking protective and angry, and (dare I say) HOT! Is that wrong of me? The guy had obviously drunk too much because he took a swing and when he missed, Tom rocked him right across his jaw. The drunk guy flew backward and Tom turned around and asked, "So you ladies want to get out of here?" All casual like that, as if he didn't just lay someone out in the middle of a crowded dance floor.

Claire and I must've laughed for five straight minutes while recalling the story over and over on the way to our next destination. It was too funny but also a shock. I can't believe he stood up for me in that type of way. I've never, NEVER had a fight break out on my account, especially in the middle of dancing. *What just happened?* After that, we went to a really great steakhouse to eat some killer grub, and then we hit the Palace Casino. I won $145 on Roulette and that rounded out (no pun intended) our amazing night! I'm going to bed now because Tom's been out for 20 minutes, and I'm loving sleeping next to this handsome, strong man.

CHAPTER 13

After our little afternoon escapade yesterday, I was hesitant to leave the house when Liam asked to see me for a late lunch. I did not know if Anthony was going to pop in unannounced while I was out and wonder why I was away. I suspect he is already questioning why I was lounging around on the telephone in the middle of the day when he surprised me. He did not come home last night, so why did I stay shut up in this godforsaken house all evening? I could have had a nice, intellectually stimulating meal with a friend. Instead, I sat at home watching television all night. I could not even stay focused on the programs I stared blankly at. I just kept asking myself *why?* Why am I friends with a person like Liam and married to a person like Anthony? I should have gone to dinner last night. I should have left the one who has tried to turn my heart cold. I should have left him behind and had a wonderful time with the man who makes my heart race.

I should have, I could have. Old habits die hard, as they say. Ironically, I will be the one to die if I cannot break these old habits of mine. Habits that keep me up all night waiting for a husband that only brings me down.

I just talked to Tee, and he postponed our plans for tomorrow night. He said we would go out in a few days. "Perhaps on Saturday," he told me. I don't have plans for the weekend yet, so I said it was okay. He sounded different. A little detached, maybe? I'm sure he's just stressed from work. I mean, being a lawyer must be very demanding. I have a problem, though. I know Tom and I haven't been dating for very long, but I still find myself constantly wondering if I should stop seeing Tee. The longer I spend dangling myself between them, the more difficult it will become to keep up this facade. And the fact that I slept with Tom just reinforces that I shouldn't be with Tee at all. I can't sleep with them both. That would be ultra-deceptive of me even if we haven't had "the talk" yet. I have until the weekend to mill it over, and I'm grateful for that. I have no idea what I'm going to say to break things off with Tee. There are only so many dates that a man will take you on before he *expects* to get laid. I have to let one of them go, and I think my libido already made my decision for me.

It was Shakespeare who wrote that "sad hours seem long." Do they ever. I am torn between reality and fantasy, walking a tightrope with no safety net below to catch me, should I fall. *When I fall.* Are there spectators? Only a few. Most got bored with this dramatic circus long ago. My mother, for one. My sister. Daddy. Friends. All gone.

"First his alcoholism will ruin his life. Then it will come after yours. Or perhaps vice versa with the way it is beginning to look." Sue had already jumped ship at that point, and I suppose my mother was tossing around the idea of cutting me off as well. I understand why they left me. At first, I was angry and hurt about their abandonment. But as time went on, I began to see their point. There was a part of me that was happy I no longer had to answer to them. I didn't have to hide things from them anymore. Life became nothing more than a chain reaction of negative consequences, all stemming from his alcoholism. It was exhausting to endure, but what was really tiring was trying to keep up appearances around unsuspecting loved ones. Worse than that was being spirited around loved ones who *knew.* I always felt like a fraud.

In the beginning, I kept it strictly to myself. I would stay away from my family after a beating, maybe take a sporadic vacation to hide the truth from them. When the marks were not visible, I would go on social outings. As bad times became more frequent, I began to withdraw from everyone around us. I went out of my way to hide it. Not that I was ever much of an extrovert in the first place, but the people who knew me best could see the difference in my personality. When I did come around, I wasn't pleasant company to keep. It was too much to endure.

One day, my skirt slipped up above a bruise, and my sister questioned me. After a very persistent argument, I gave in and told her the truth. I downplayed the abuse a bit. Deep down, I thought that Anthony was a wonderful man. That this was a temporary issue, something we could fix. Sue began spending more time with me, and our mother questioned our close relationship that started out of the blue. Of course, we were always close, but we didn't spend every day together before. She knew there was something wrong, and I forbade my sister from confiding in our mother. When Sue begged me to tell her the truth and I still refused, the secret put a strain on their relationship. Susie started to withdraw from our family, just as I had. Instead of going to family events, she would stay with me. Of course, the violence progressed to the point of no return. It could no longer be our little secret as it increasingly became obvious to more and more around us. Some of our mutual friends knew, and I could not blame them at all for phasing us out of their circles. Some of them probably questioned if the stories were even true. He has always been so good at fooling everyone, but Anthony's rage is also incredibly unpredictable. One day, I suddenly realized we were no longer surrounded by friends.

The more my family tried to talk me out of my commitment to him, the more I concretely stood by my husband. I was blinded by (what I thought was) love. I always saw his potential. That was my gigantic flaw in our love story and its demise. It held me here next to him for so damn long. I fantasized he could rise to be the kind of man *I thought he was* underneath that hard exterior of his. But as Maya Angelou said, "When someone shows you who they are, believe them the first time." He can never become what I *made up* as his potential and magically gain characteristics that *never existed* within him. I set a bar that couldn't be met because it was based on an imaginary person I'd never really known.

As my family grew more upset about my marital situation, it ruled my sister's life. It got to the point that she was neglecting my niece and nephew. She was so emotionally drained and consumed by my depression that she started taking it out on her own family. When my sister began avoiding my calls, my mom broke the heartbreaking news to me that my life had become "too much" for my sister.

"Too dangerous, unpredictable. Suzie is sorry, honey." That was one of the last times I spoke with my mother. It was right before my father's death. And here I am, still paying the price. And for what? The bad has certainly outweighed the good for many years now. Why have I never left and contacted the people who really cared for me? Foolish pride, for one. Sometimes I stare at the phone and will it to ring, yearning to hear my mother's voice on the other end, but it never does.

Having a full social life is fun and all, but I need to set aside time for my artwork. My canvas is actually collecting dust. Literal dust. I had such a cool idea for an exhibit. It's expensive, though. Okay. So I want to take TVs and have black and white pictures rotating on the screens every minute or so. I want to paint, like, 50% of each screen in color to coordinate with the different pics. Sounds righteous to me. And confusing, I think, when I tried to explain it. I was just throwing around ideas, and Tom belly laughed at me. No surprise there. He doesn't even like Picasso. Ridiculous, so ridiculous. He's beyond help. His opinion of art doesn't even count, as far as I'm concerned.

The only problem with my exhibit is I have nowhere to

actually exhibit it. Combined with the fact that I don't have a black and white television (or several) to completely ruin for no reason at all. It's kind of discouraging, this whole starving artist life. I did paint today for the first time in a while, and my work is way more cheerful than it was previously. Super vibrant colors combined with simplistic images. Not dark and intricate like the last ones. It's funny how I'll have an idea completely worked out in my head, but it *always* comes out differently than I had planned. It's also really interesting how my mood is so relevant to what ends up being created. When I'm angry, which isn't very often, I use more black and red. When I'm happy, I use more vibrant yellows and pastels. I didn't know anything about this before I started experimenting with art. When I let my "creative juices" flow freely, I let go of all of my feelings and just let my hands do what they want. Other times, I feel like I have to channel my emotions to get anything accomplished at all. I feed off of whatever mood I'm in. Once, when I was mad, I put on this old Korn song that says:

I HATE YOU

I HATE YOU

I HATE YOU

I put it on repeat and just fed that anger over and over and over. But my anger fed my artwork and, in the end, I had something really great in front of me. And you know what? It made me feel so much better after I was finished, too – like some sort of release. Art is a wonderful thing. I'm so glad I found it.

I need to see Sandra. With my life being packed full of fun lately, I may be neglecting my friendship. I call her here and there, but she really needs to get out for a good time more often. I'll invite her to dinner, and maybe we can do something fun after. I want to make sure she knows someone cares about her.

Tiffany called just as I was thumbing through the obituaries. About twice a week I go through them, mostly looking for my mother's name – always praying that it's not there. I halfheartedly wonder if she does the same for me. We are alike in a lot of ways. Daddy is probably watching from above, shaking his head in disappointment at our mutual silent treatment. I could pick up the phone and call at any time but until I improve my situation, I cannot expect to have a decent conversation with her. I cannot expect her to stand beside me when she made it clear years ago she emphatically would not.

What I would give to hear the sweet resonance in her voice, the encouragement she always had to offer. And what would I say to her? "Hello, mother. Yes, yes. I'm still living with a horrible monster, but would you like to grab lunch this afternoon? Just let me touch up the concealer for my eye, and we'll hit the little sushi bar down on Broadway." I can already hear the deafening silence of the call ending.

Claire, CeeCee, and I are all really excited. Carl is leaving next Friday after work to go on his fishing trip, so we are already making plans for 7:00 o'clock that night. Sleepover! Girls weekend! At least for three blissful days, I won't have to worry about who to go out with or what I'm going to do. No work. No boys. No stress. What more could a girl want?

CHAPTER 14

Sometimes, I feel I am being watched.

While I am at work, there is always a high volume of people around. At any given moment, there could be several different individuals glancing in my direction. From fellow employees to customers, their eyes beg for assistance, should we make even the slightest contact. Even a stranger's stare can, for a moment, be *felt* by an individual before it is seen. This is *not* what I'm speaking of. Lately, I feel as though someone is literally lurking behind every corner just out of sight. Is it completely insane to think a person can be followed from the front? I think it's entirely possible, especially if the victim's schedule never varies. Like mine. People like me are predictable targets. Dependable. All I have done lately is spend time at home and go to work, per usual. That may be the problem. I've had the same schedule at Binded for two years now. Anyone who comes into the store on even a semi-regular basis knows my schedule. I am often referenced by name as customers speak to other employees about past purchases, special orders, or recommendations. I *always* park in the same area of the parking lot. Standing in front of the store and facing the lot, my Lexus is in the farthest left row and about halfway down the aisle. I should stop thinking this way. My paranoid thoughts would take over my life if I let them. If I start parking in a different area, am I letting my paranoia take control of me? Or is it considered a smart move? I am going to do it, vary my routine a bit. I'll park in a different spot. Talk about walking on the wild side, right? That way, if some creep is waiting for me to show up in that left row every single day, at least I've given myself a chance.

Of course, if someone knows my car, this is all a moot point. He can always wait for me after I am off my shift. It is typically dark when I leave. I think I should make a purchase before my next shift. I will outfit my keyring with pepper spray or Mace. I need to start protecting myself. If I cannot protect myself inside my own home, I should at least start trying to while I'm outside of it. But which poses the most danger, in reality? My own husband or a sociopathic stranger? It feels as if they are one and the same.

When I talked to Sandra today, she freaked out on me a little. I asked her if she wanted to go to dinner, and she said that it sounded like a great idea. She started blabbing on and on about changing her routine and that "he" couldn't follow her from the front if he didn't know where she was going.

"Could he?" She questioned me, in a challenging tone.

I kinda mumbled an "uh-huh" here and there, but I wondered what in the hell my friend was talking about. What in the fuck is "following someone from the front" anyway? I've never heard of that shit before. Don't you have to be behind someone to follow them? Ummmm... Is Sandra okay? I'm relieved we have plans later. She sounded a little frantic. I hope she is just busy and overwhelmed. I did call her during her shift at work. Speaking of work, I think I'm going to look for another job.

Requirements:
Good pay
Decent people

NO pervy boss

I'm beyond over the perviness at work. Claire is practically begging me not to quit and leave her alone with the wolves. There aren't many people in the office that she gets along with besides me – and vice versa, actually. There are only two other females our age, and they're both complete bitches from hell –

That's where they said they were from, right? Hell? But really, I'm talking about straight-up whores. Who prances around bending over in front of other people's husbands trying to entice them? Who does that? Anyone who deliberately tries to tempt, date, or fuck a married man is a complete and total ho. End of story, period. There are, like, BILLIONS of men in the world. You're telling me you don't find any of those other guys attractive, and you have to have this *one* that's already taken? I'm not buying it. Home-wrecking whores. Just my opinion. Take it or leave it. And when the wives find out, these bitches always have the same tired lines. "If you kept your husband satisfied." Or the copout, "If he didn't do it with me, he would've done it with someone else." No, bitch. You're just evil.

Do you know what I say? Once a cheater, always a cheater. This kinda shit makes me wonder why more women aren't like Lorena Bobbit. You remember old girl, Lorena, right? Caught her husband cheating, and she straight cut that man's dick off. I'm pretty sure she threw it into a field, too. Don't you think if more men knew their cocks would be forcibly removed and deposited at high speeds into a dark field as a consequence for their pig-headed ways, they would think twice before getting their dicks wet by a cheap piece of passerby pussy? DAMN RIGHT, THEY WOULD. What? Just saying. Imagine it, though. Men start getting a complex, too scared to cheat anymore. Always wondering if they will face the literal Peter Eater as consequence. I'm fucking dead. What was my point, even?

Oh yeah, Claire won't have any friends left because this shithole office is filled to the brim with hoes. She'll have plenty of friends outside of A & A Chemicals, but what fun is going to work if you don't have someone on the inside to shoot the shit with? What do you do if you're having a terrible day, for whatever reason, and there's no one to vent to? Who will she complain about Carl to every other week? Who will she share all the juicy details with when they make up? All of this was part of her actual argument trying to get me to stay working there. I mean, it's not like I'm walking out right this second, but this bitch laying out her whole defense acting like her life depends on my job.

"I've still got to find another place to work and put in my notice," I reassured her. "It's not like I'm walking out right this second."

Unless I get a quick and easy job working with Sandra at Binded Books. I've already met her boss, and she would probably enjoy the company. And then I could keep an eye on her. Lately, I've had a really bad feeling in the pit of my stomach when I think about my friend. Her marital problems are so out of control, and now she is sounding a little crazy. It would make things a lot better if she would just leave her jackass husband. Or at least Lorena Bobbit him!

Dinner with Tiffany was just what I needed to snap my mind back to reality and out of the dark thoughts I've been consumed by. Sometimes, reality is not the easiest place to reside in, but it is the best option we've got. I would rather live in reality and take a little vacation in a fantasy world than the other way around. My mother used to say something quite often after she learned of my abusive relationship. It was a little different every time she brought it up, but it always contained the same message.

"It's a nice piece of real estate," she would talk of the state hospital, pointing up at the ghostly white building with black windows next to the interstate. On another occasion, "You should invest in some stock. Maybe focus on the healthcare industry, pharmaceuticals, or maybe a hospital." This, to an outsider, could seem like a normal conversation, but my mother was trying to remind me of my circumstances. I could potentially be utilizing those services regularly. If I stayed in my abusive relationship with an alcoholic, I could very well end up in a mentally-impaired state or with permanent physical disabilities.

It's been a whole decade since those conversations, and I've never thought she was correct about that state hospital bit until today. Am I going crazy? Thinking I am being watched. Thinking someone is following me. Thinking I am in danger from a person I've yet to prove into existence or even witness at all, yet I willingly walk back into an unsafe environment every single time I step over my own threshold.

My mother was right. I have got to be losing my damn mind. I suppose one could argue that if I *realize* I am losing my mind, I must still have some grasp of sanity, right? Certainly, an insane person would believe their fantasies to be a reality and, therefore, would not label themselves as mentally unfit. Thinking your fantasies to be reality would simply label it a new reality, would it not? This would brand something twice as farfetched as a new fantasy, bringing this new reality farther and farther from the plane of normalcy that everyone around you resides on in the real world – whatever "real" *really is* anyway. I should stop. This kind of thinking is exactly the reason I realize I am, in fact, not losing it. I'm sitting here spoon-feeding the insanity. Adding fuel to the fire. I twirl around in my own crazy thoughts and confuse myself, making me start to question things all over again. What kind of person confuses themself in their own head?

Back to dinner. It was wonderfully uneventful. I hadn't realized how much I was missing Tiffany until I saw her in the flesh. She was absolutely glowing. Immediately, I felt my eyes open up clearly and my tense shoulders relax. Talking with her made my sadness positively melt away, at least for a moment. I felt ridiculous telling her about my imaginary worries at work. Even if it did sound stupid, she was still concerned about my safety. She mentioned she may apply for a job at Binded. It sounded more like a fleeting thought than a genuine intention, but it would be nice to have her lovely face around more often. I would feel bad for her friend at her current company. If Tiffany leaves, it sounds like she would be without any allies and surrounded by virtual molesters. But from what Tiff has said about Claire, she sounds like she can handle herself just fine. She definitely sounds like a confident and strong woman.

Compared to me, though, who isn't?

CHAPTER 15

I had a great idea tonight after dinner with Sandra. She said she's paranoid, but I realized she's really just scared, in general. I think she is fearful of her husband. That terrifying feeling that used to only grip ahold of her at home is now leaking into her life outside in the real world.

"You should take a self-defense class for women. We could take it together!" I suggested excitedly. "Yeeeessss, San, we can learn how to beat ass together for real!" Because *who needs to Lorena Bobbit when you can execute a proper chokehold?* They have one class at the community center by my apartment complex, and it's really cheap for the whole course. It's available for people who live outside my county boundaries, too. Sandra and I definitely don't stay in the same zip code, with her fancy self. I know she has plenty of money, but I want to pay for this class. I don't want her husband wondering about the charge, but I would also love to show my support for her and her personal growth. I will do everything I can to build her up and help her find the inner strength I know she is capable of. *I will not abandon you, my friend.* I know it's hard for her to leave him, so I will stick around as long as it takes. I thought about my commitment to her as we parted ways. She agreed she would think about it and get back to me about the class.

I'll ask Claire if she wants to join us, too. Everyone should know at least the basics of self-defense, myself included. I don't know the first thing about this stuff. Sandra acted like she has to give it some thought, but I've decided she doesn't really have a choice. I will find a way to get her to go. I hope it doesn't end up being a battle, though. I'm not trying to have it come to that, but I definitely don't plan on backing down about this.

Tiffany phoned and proposed Claire, her, and I all take the self-defense class together, and she wants to treat all of us and take care of the cost. I had said I would consider it, but she argued with me.

"There's no time to think. The first class starts in an hour. We'll pick you up in 30 minutes. See you soon. Wear comfy clothes!" Click. She hung up on me, that little wench! I laughed a little to myself, as there's really no point in arguing with her about this. If I really, REALLY didn't want her to pick me up, I know she would respect that. I also know that spending time with these ladies and learning how to fight should be numero uno on my priority list. It's nice to have a friend who has my best interest in mind. Lending ideas and advice that could potentially save my life someday, whether in the house or out. Hopefully, I'll never have to put into practice what I'm taught, but I pray it will give me the boost of confidence I so desperately need.

So here I am. An abused spouse, mentally willing to be physically prepared. What a step in the right direction! A renewed sense of purpose, and it's amazing to feel like the light at the end of the tunnel is looming closer. I've weaved my way through a deep, dark course for many years, and Tiffany happened upon me in my very weakest moment. Or was it actually the birth of my strongest moment? Either way, I am so grateful for the light she brings to my journey.

I cannot fathom where my story will go – what direction life will take me – but as I lined up for that first class, I glanced at Tiffany and Claire in utter disbelief. For the first time, I can feel myself nearing the end of this difficult uphill battle I've been on. I can feel the energy swirling around me, a plot forming in the Universe, thick and dripping with anticipation.

I try to concentrate on my task at hand as the instructor begins, "How do attackers choose their victims? Their posture, demeanor, and the way they walk." I squared my posture with feigned confidence and listened intently. She was captivating, and I stared in awe at how strong she seemed, ingesting every single word she uttered as if my life depended on it.

I guess you could say that self-defense class was a "hit!" Ha! Just one class had Sandra waltzing around like a brand new woman, already standing taller in her petite frame. It was amazing to see an instant change. Learning simple, effective moves made her burn with a mighty fire I've never seen in her before. I saw such determination and concentration as she perfectly executed one move after another. From the moment we met, Sandra's eyes have spoken only sadness, fear, and a vague spark of hope from time to time. But never determination. Never strength or confidence. Resolve. Sure, she is strong to put up with that asshat all these years, no one would doubt that. She's been surviving. Today, though, she was *thriving,* and it was such a beautiful thing to witness. If you ask me, she should run straight from her husband's arms into that private detective's. Just saying, she gets real flustered when she talks about him.

"Why are you blushing?" I teased her after she mentioned him. Of course, I would never encourage her to cheat on her spouse even if he *is* a wife-beating douchebag. She denied a romantic interest in Liam, admitting they talk regularly, but it is a platonic and professional relationship. Maybe Sandra doesn't realize how she looks when she talks about this P.I. guy. I'll have to leave her to figure it out on her own. She's a grown-ass woman. Eventually, she will realize if she wants him in some type of way. Maybe this incognito crush will encourage her to leave Anthony, and I'm all for that shit. Anyway, she definitely doesn't need dating advice from me. I'm as confused and indecisive as they come, bordering on commitment-phobic myself. She doesn't look down on me like I am younger or inexperienced, so I *could* offer advice, but I honestly don't think it would be helpful. Sandra has been receiving unsolicited advice for years. Right now, she needs an unconditional friend to listen to her and remain supportive in whatever decisions she moves forward with. I mean, that's exactly what has been lacking in her life for a decade. I can't even imagine how isolating that must've felt for her.

.

Sometimes I wonder about Anthony. I don't wonder if he is a great man, or if he is going to conquer some kind of outstanding feat of selflessness to better mankind. I already know those answers. I ponder less worldly questions, such as: when my husband does not come home for days on end – which is becoming all too frequent, in between odd bouts of sporadic lovemaking – how does he return with a different outfit on? I understand the obvious answer is that he changes his clothes. I have questions. How does he get them? Does he keep a suitcase in his Jag or at the office and occasionally launder them? Does he constantly spend outrageous amounts of money on new clothing, pretending this is a normal first-world privilege? Does he decide to stay out with leggy blondes last minute, or does he pack in anticipation of these occasions?

Maybe leggy blonde isn't the only woman he is seeing. Maybe he has a whole other secret life with a whole different wardrobe. Who knows? He is a stranger to me. I spoke with Liam last night, and he has been trailing Anthony. Blondie ended up being his secretary, how unoriginal and cliché of him. As strange as it may sound, he said he thinks Anthony is actually following someone else. He said he's 95% positive my husband is tailing someone, and I cannot for the life of me wrap my head around that fact. Unless it's me? Am I in danger from my husband even outside of our home? If he was the reason I felt I was being watched, I have a heightened sense of nervousness about my recent activities. Liam said he will figure out who he's stalking and make sure he's not doing anything harmful. *My husband, the stalker?* No, that's preposterous. Not in his line of work. It would be an astronomical mistake. What kind of evil is he planning, and who will his next victim be? This has taken a strange turn I did not foresee.

"Stay away from that guy," was Tom's response when I told him I wasn't available to go out later. He sounded so bitter when he said it, he practically spat the words at me. He didn't have to say Tee's name for both of us to know who he was referring to. Of course, Tom didn't know for a fact I was seeing Tee later, but I guess it's pretty obvious. He's the one who introduced us, after all. If Tom wants to keep seeing me, he needs to drop this territorial, jealous act and realize I am a grown woman who decides who is worthy of my time. While I defiantly got ready for my date, it hurt a little to know Tom's arms wouldn't be wrapped around me later.

CHAPTER 16

Liam stopped by for an hour or so. He followed Anthony and another woman to the theater, so he knew the coast was clear. He probably came by because he pities me. The poor little wifey, sitting at home while her husband treats a younger woman to a nice evening on the town. Surely it's the life I deserve, but I have all but given up my right to be treated like a lady. I've conditioned my husband throughout this entire miserable marriage that I am not only unworthy of respect, but I'm unworthy of even the tiniest speck of gratitude.

The way I am beginning to see things – and clearly, for the first time – is that Anthony has been taking me for granted since I entered adulthood. I have cooked, fantastically. I have cleaned, immaculately. And he has never even muttered a thank you. I have given up on my personal goals like the good little codependent he expected me to become.

The words of the instructor echoed in my memory, *"How do they choose their victims?"* He saw in me the promise of lifelong servitude and unwavering commitment. My dreams died. My goals were forgotten. And for what? *To journal this abusive cycle year after year, repeating how suffocating and exhausting this life is, in spiral notebooks. Every year's notebook cast away at the end of it, defeating any lingering sense of hope or resolve, as each new and shiny journal is cracked open, masquerading as a fresh start.*

Fifteen years has felt as if it were fifty. I finally believe I have the right to complain, to speak up, to be heard. *To change.* I have finally been beaten *out of* submission. Perhaps I've already passed the point of insanity. Should I pull back the reins or continue down this path of surefire destruction? I am becoming as unpredictable as my husband these days. A prisoner of my own mind, I've begun twisting devious and intricate stories of revenge and cannot help but get caught up in the allure of it all.

For example just yesterday, I thought that a prisoner sure sounds entertaining. This ridiculous, bright white bedroom shines at me, mockingly, as I recall all the immoral deeds that have played out here. The walls practically beg me to destroy them, to strip them bare, and shatter everything hanging peacefully upon them. Just like the silly pipe dreams of naïve little girls, I want to squash everything in this room. This disgusting bedroom. Fuck this space. Wait, maybe I will keep it beautiful upstairs for the sake of appearances. Yes, it's better I keep my prisoner in the basement like a proper guard.

He's constantly ridiculing me. I picture myself in front of him with a clown mask on. Anthony isn't scared of clowns like so many others. *I'll make sure he's scared of them after my games.* Yes, a prisoner. But wait! Shall my prisoner be free to roam the windowless basement or kept locked away like my delicious little secret for the remainder of his days? What jealousy would be felt in the heart of my dear guest, while constantly hearing the creak of floorboards above his head, as I move about at my leisure? The chills from the drafty corners of a vast, dark basement. Not being allowed to go further than his chains allow, should I choose that route.

Will he recognize that the sound of running water never fades? I've jostled the toilet handle to make sure it's constantly attempting to fill the bowl, never quite managing to succeed. It runs day in and day out, a consistent reminder of the luxuries being withheld. And as you long for a glistening porcelain toilet because you know your own sits just out of reach, you'll realize all of your past mistakes. You've never known a longing quite as strong as this, and you think about your transgressions as urine soaks the cold and unforgiving floor around you. *Again.* The stench of your own shit will surround you like it's your muse. But it's not. Because it is mine. The sound reverberates through your head at all hours. How many days of hearing that damn toilet run? The tape around your limbs is unaffected by the elements. Don't worry, it is a strong brand. I made sure to check the reviews. I hate you even more than I could ever really convey through these efforts. My plan will not waiver, my love, my dearest hostage. I will transport all of the lovely photos from our bedroom down to the basement, so you will never feel lonely. Occasionally, I will grace you with my presence. Feed you some scraps to sustain your life. Pretend we are a happy couple. Just like you do when you dress up and put on a show for the outside world.

Run my finger along your jugular. Just a friendly reminder.

I
Am
Now
In
Control
Here
Darling.

And while my *hypothetical* prisoner struggles and cries and begs for mercy I've no longer the will to lend, I will lovingly take his hands in mine and apologize. Over and over again, I will apologize. How much time will pass before he stops believing and takes only my actions as my word? Months? Years? Or will he crumble after merely a few days of empty remorse? An apology is but a word or two. It's quite simple, really. In the grocery store, we mumble it in passing. When someone leans in front of you to grab the last can of albacore tuna – finally on sale for once – they recite the phrase without even making eye contact. They *knew* you were going for that can so why even bother with empty apologies? Why say it if it is not even heartfelt? To free themselves of the guilt, that's why. To live another day without the conscience knowing that you are a waste of fucking space here, haphazardly blowing through life taking advantage of anyone you please.

"THAT WAS MY ALBACORE, BITCH!" I want to scream at her. *Is she even planning to eat that tonight?* But I refrain. I leave the store and stop at another location to get my can of tuna. It doesn't taste as good as I'd hoped, but I'm still happy I went out of my way for it. So I have decided if I ever keep Anthony locked in the basement for an extended period of time, I will be sure to look him straight in his eyes when I apologize. I will make sure I don't mumble at all so he will know that I really, *really* mean it. It will mean so much more that way. *It will be special.* Unless I do it for, say – I don't know – ten years straight. *What would it mean then?* I'm just going to take a gander at this one, but I theorize someone could go absolutely mad if they were subjected to such a life. *Absolutely mad!* And they may even want to die.

Is it possible to become over-confident in self-defense class? I think that's my current situation.

"I dare someone to fuck with me!" I concluded loudly. "Three pounds of pressure to pull off a human ear? Fuck yes, I can't wait!" I probably shouldn't be like this with only two classes under my belt, but this is invigorating and life-altering shit we're doing here! A few years ago, I took Taekwondo for a month. I remember only one thing from 12 classes: how to break free when someone grabs your wrists. Nothing else stuck with me after I was finished with that month, so it was pointless for me to continue learning their choreographed routines for belt promotion. With this, I feel like I'm absorbing techniques that anyone, big or small, can understand and implement easily. None of that pointless Karate Kid "wax on, wax off" bullshit. Jamming noses, kicking crotches, and biting off bits of flesh are all endorsed tactics in this session, and I'm about that life. All I can say is that someone is in for a pretty big surprise if they grab my wrist after today. Three pounds of pressure, bitch.

I am, as Tiffany would say, abso-fucking-lutely FED UP. I am sick and tired of waiting for my husband to come home so I can walk on a tightrope, constantly wondering if I'm going to be treated or tricked. Will he keep his filthy paws to himself today? Will he wrap them around my neck or use them to kindly caress me back into submission?

I'm calling Liam. I want a night out, and I know he can keep me safe, even if I am being followed by some nutcase. It's too late now, anyway. Either Anthony knows I'm branching out into new avenues or he doesn't. Who cares anymore? I'm leaving him. I'm a woman, and I demand to be treated as such. By someone, at least. Even if it's platonic. I'm aware I am just a client. This is not out of any kind of romantic intent on my part, and Liam respects our professional boundaries. Although, I have found myself longing for more than a simple meeting. And there was that moment he flashed through my mind as my husband touched me. Okay. That was actually twice. But given my circumstances, a Freudian slip here and there is entirely normal. Right?

Maybe I will fire him tonight. Is that a crazy idea? I would much rather he just discontinue his pursuit of additional evidence against Anthony. It will serve no good, as I'm steadfast in my resolve to get out from under his rule no matter what. I need this man in a pure way. He is a source of genuine comfort to me. Friendship. Someone to teach me to trust again. Someone I'm not afraid of. That is my true desire. I don't need someone reporting all of my husband's wrongdoings, as his devotion has never really been in question. I have finally allowed myself to fully come to terms with it. My "better half" is a threat to my happiness and my future.

I wish I could meet Liam on a more personal level without the filter of professionalism. Each time I gaze upon his charming smile, I am transfixed. His eyes pry into my very soul like no one I've ever had the privilege to be in the presence of. I mean, I would not get involved with him while I'm under Anthony's roof. That would be entirely inappropriate. Soon he will cease being a hired employee. I admit I am interested to see how our conversations will evolve after tonight's meeting. *Was there a spark between us the first time we met? The day you resolved to protect me.* Because he was contractually obligated, I reminded myself during our imaginary interlude. Make-believe Sandra is quite assertive.

When I went out with Tee the other night, I had an awesome time. He dragged me around from place to place, spoiling and entertaining me at every turn. And I broke it off at the end of the night! Well, I tried to break it off. I think I did, but it seems weird to admit that I'm not really sure that's how it went. All I thought about the entire night was Tom. I was out with an amazing, confident, handsome, loaded man, and all I wanted to do was run away and find my way into Tom's strong and comforting embrace. I want to rush back to him so he can hold me tightly and keep me safe from the rest of the world.

Sure, there were moments during our date that Tom slipped away from my thoughts, but he always came jolting back into my brain. I'm not really sure what went wrong when I tried to explain to Tee that I didn't want to see him anymore. I told him he is a great guy – blah, blah, blah – and I'm having some personal issues that I need to sort through on my own. Some more blah, blah, blah. And I also told him there was no chance of us moving on to that "next level" in our relationship, so we should just cut ties now. We chatted for a little more and then at the end, he told me he would call me. *Wait, what?* I was really shocked. It's almost as if he disregarded the entire convo where I rejected him. Was he confused? It was pretty point-blank. I've never broken it off with someone and walked away wondering if we were still together. How did I miss the whole negotiation phase of this deal? Is this because he's a lawyer? Sneaky bastard. If he does call, I'm going to make it crystal clear this relationship is O-V-E-R.

I just hope it's not too late to save things with Tom. He is such a good guy for me, and I will be so upset if he doesn't want to be with me after this. I know I shouldn't have gone out with Tee, but I needed to work through this whole process to be sure. I've seen the light now! I was scared and that's okay. I'll be honest with Tom and stern with Tee.

"GRRRRR LEAVE ME ALONE, TEE!" I really should practice. He's crafty. I can do that. Easy peasy. Can't talk me into things I don't want. I'm super strong, self-defense Tiff. Yes, I can do this! I think.

What can I say about Detective Hanson? I truly *believed* we were friends. My heart has been met with a tragic consequence it didn't anticipate. What have I done? It seems he feels he should not, in fact, be in my company now that I no longer require his investigative services. I have lost him on all fronts. I thought he held genuine care for me and our blooming friendship, but it just wasn't true. What have I done?

I begged him, crying and sobbing uncontrollably, to reconsider, "Please, don't do this to me!" I couldn't possibly live without this man in my life. I admit it, okay? The warmth that his presence affords me, the comfort and wholesome conversation he brings, I don't want it to end. He said that Anthony would eventually find out we were friends and, whether platonic or more, we would be met with a fury he preferred not to face. He's right. No matter if we could maintain a pure friendship or not, it would put both of our lives in jeopardy. My life is already in jeopardy, though. Doesn't he care about that at all? I was genuinely surprised. I really thought I mattered to him. I obviously constructed some kind of connection between us that didn't actually exist. I feel like I need him so badly, right down to my very core – my soul aches for him, my heart yearns. My blood whispers his name with every pump. Can this be possible? How did I conjure such a feeling alone? I have never felt more stupid in all my life.

"It's just a friendship," I argued with him. It was a last-ditch effort, and the pain in my voice dripped with desperate emotion, tears still streaming down my cheeks. Even I didn't believe my argument.

Leave him, she whispered in my head. SHUT UP, MOTHER.

How do I leave when I've stayed so long? How do I leave?

Leave him, or you will pay with your life. GET OUT OF MY HEAD!

Where will I go? I'm going mad. Loneliness constricts me. I feel like I can't breathe. I need freedom. I need allies.

So leave him, and your allies will come. IF YOU DON'T TALK TO ME IN REAL LIFE, WHY ARE YOU IN MY HEAD SO DAMN OFTEN?

Is it possible? Could I leave so soon? I'm so unprepared. Where? Where would I go? Would Liam talk to me again if I left Anthony? If I threw myself at his mercy, would he choose me or would walk away again? I'm not going to make it much longer here. I'm – I'm so defeated. So broken. I just can't anymore. I'm too tired.

I went to Binded and filled out an employment

application. I need to get out of this fucked-up company, and Sandra seems like she's losing her damn mind. Her private investigator friend and she aren't speaking anymore, which I personally feel is really shitty of him. Everyone that woman has ever put her trust in has let her down. I know it's because she is with that raging dickfuck hubby of hers, but it still sucks that Liam won't talk to her anymore. So what if she had a schoolgirl crush on this guy? Who cares? Nothing happened between them, so I think he's tossing away a potentially amazing friendship because his job ended. I guess he's just a huge wuss. Whatever. Men seriously suck so bad.

CHAPTER 17

How I long for formal education. A degree would be such a nice thing to possess. Being taught how to defend myself has reminded me exactly how much I enjoy learning. I still remember the look on my mother's face when I told her I was going to wed Anthony and put my pursuit of journalism "on hold." Her eyes, to my surprise, did not even narrow in anger. Nor did they register surprise. They are only filled with sorrow. Pity.

She stared deep into my face when she questioned me through her clenched jaw, "Did Anthony talk you into giving up your lifelong dream, child? Was this his idea?" She always seemed to like him up to that point. Maybe she only tolerated him, and I never realized it. Now his name was forced through pursed lips, dripping like poison, and hanging there heavily in the air between us. Was I blind up to that point about my mother's real opinion of my mate?

Opinions are formed in the first minute you meet someone, and it amazes me how steadfast you can become in that belief. Had I missed something in my mother's initial assessment of Anthony? No matter how falsely you have someone pegged, you've already formed a strong opinion of them. Of strangers. The way they look, dress, talk, move, their haircut. From trivial things, mostly. Nothing that speaks of their true character. When someone runs you off the road because they're too frugal to spring for a hands-free phone adaptor, it is automatically assumed they are a horrible person. Sometimes, that one incident can follow someone around and ruin their entire day or even their life. Everything that goes wrong after that moment, for the next 12 hours, is that other driver's fault because they caused the start of a crappy day for you. *Everything was fine until they almost ran you off the road. That asshole!* In a split second, you rage, feeling pure unabridged hatred for a complete stranger, without knowing anything about them at all.

Yet, some of those same people return home daily to their abusive mate. They put up with so much more than accidentally being run off the road. And willingly, to boot. Angry at the stranger for cutting them off but coming home to an evil spouse, and they still cite it is love.

What if we treated others with the same resolve?

They cut you off, and you still love them.

They cut you off again, and your car goes down an embankment. You still love them.

It starts rolling. And flipping. And bursts into flames. You continue loving them.

This stranger you continue to love notices your pain, and he runs down the embankment to bring you up the steep hill to safety. He finally saved you! He sees your love for him!

And then he runs you off the road again. Down the embankment, you roll. *Again and again.*

But...

But...

But...

You *still* love him. Shouldn't that be enough? Doesn't he recognize how much you love him? We can hate a stranger that accidentally runs us into another lane ONE TIME, yet continually and willingly take abuse from those closest to us. *How backward is that thinking?* My mother had obviously known what kind of person Anthony was long before he ever raised a hand to me. She saw what I wouldn't allow myself to see. She called him out on his manipulative ways in front of people, and now I live my days with him and without her. Just like he wanted.

I have never been so upset in all my life. Tee had the audacity to go to Caesar's and *threaten Tom* about seeing me. What in the actual fuck? Is he a nut job or what? I cannot believe this even happened. He is a lawyer, for God's sake! We never even *fucked*. Get over it, bro. Acting like I'm a piece of property to claim possession of. Exactly who does this motherfucker think he is anyway? He should definitely know better in his line of work. You can't just go around harassing people. I think Tom should call the police and file paperwork or something. Anything except what he's doing which is *absolutely nothing!*

"At least get an order of protection, so he can't come to your place of employment anymore," I pleaded with my new boyfriend. It would be a hell of a lot easier on me, too, because now I'm nervous to hang around Caesar's in case Tee decides to be crazy again. I'm legit scared!

Oh em gee. *My boyfriend.* It sounds so weird!

Back to the matter at hand. I think the old boy is losing it. We went out a few times, that's all. I thought he was normal and great, and I broke it off in a really simple, straightforward way. I didn't see this coming at all. He's like a completely different person. Dr. Jekyll and Mr. Hyde. If Tom won't do anything about it, maybe I can. Or am I just blowing this out of proportion? Tom seems pretty proud of himself. Why does he have that look painted across his face? Oh geez, I get it. He is winning some kind of imaginary, macho-man contest against Tee. Tom got the girl. Oh my goodness. Men are ridiculous!

"Okay, Tom. Take your pretend, man-trophy home, honey. Good job," I praised him, sarcastically, but he was still grinning like a damn fool. I need to talk to Sandra. If there is anything she would have a strong opinion on, it's a crazy man. She lives in a house filled with drama much worse than this. It's time for a man-bashing session, so I will swoop her earlier than normal before class. That way, we can chat for a few extra minutes before taking our aggression out on the air around us.

Speaking of man-bashing, the perv gave me a quarter raise per hour. *Sarcastic yayyyyyy* Maybe I should wear tighter jeans to squeeze another dime out of the miser. Claire is going to quit soon. She hasn't said that, but she keeps bringing up the lawsuit. She is so obsessed with how the pervert treats us. But he really treats everyone like that, so we're not the only ones dealing with this. He probably thinks all women are sluts because his sister is one. Or because *he* is one. He cheats and divorces, cheats, and divorces again. Maybe he's faithful now, but I highly doubt it. His wife is insanely jealous around the office, and I can tell she's not particularly fond of Claire and I. Serious resting bitch face on that one, but what did she expect when she married a cheater? Don't get me wrong, I like money as much as the next girl, but I don't like it enough to sleep with a short, fat, bald perverted man-whore. Seriously, how does Bob get so much play? Gotta be the wallet. How much money is that man really sitting on?

It sounds to me like Tiffany could be tangled up in quite a dangerous predicament. I have a very horrible feeling about that lawyer she was briefly dating. I never completely trusted him in the first place. Maybe it's because I haven't trusted male lawyers for a long time now. Why do bad men have to prey on nice people like Tiffany? And like me. I have come to a serious conclusion. I need to have a living will concretely in place. Tiff invited me out after class today, so I will need to run by my attorney's office tomorrow. At least I know I can trust her. She has held my trust money safe all these years.

If I am ever on life support, for the love of God, unplug it immediately. My life is best ended, as I'd only wake up to disappointment. I cannot imagine waking to stay here in this nightmare of a life. What would I possibly look forward to? *Congratulations! You've miraculously pulled through and made a full recovery to return to −regret and disappointment!* To fight such horrible odds and win, only to be delivered back to the losing hand that life has dealt? Not likely to be a happy reunion with a room full of loved ones. No one's kind eyes sparkling at my return; No one waiting incessantly with worry next to my bed. More likely, I'd wake to a living hell. Taking a rain check for heaven to come back to this shithole? No thanks, I'll take a hard pass on that. First thing in the morning, I will go to the attorney's office and get this paperwork completed. I feel like I'm finally taking control to secure my future, in a way. I already despise waking up almost every single day, and that is after only eight hours of slumber. How disappointing.

I can't believe the bitch did it! I'm in literal disbelief, but Claire walked out. She told the perv to kiss her "Italian ass" and just before she went out the door, she turned and added, "Just for the record, that wasn't a sexual invitation, you fucking pervert." She glanced at me and with a magical little wink, she was gone. I looked at my boss with a smirk on my face that I couldn't hide even if I tried. I put my hand in the air and gave it a little wave, grabbing his attention from across the office, like he was a server.

"Two weeks notice," I said with a gigantic smile.

CHAPTER 18

This has got to be one of the worst mornings to be out and about. After battling rush-hour accident traffic on the interstate, I finally got to my attorney's only to find the notary was out of the office on vacation. I either have to sit on my papers for a week or bring them somewhere else. The latter is out, as I trust very few people outside of my extremely tight circle. It's just as well I not think about this any longer, for it's only serving to grind on my nerves. It's not the notary I'm upset with, it's me. I should've done this years ago, and it irks me to all high hell that I'm unable to complete this task the very moment I want to. I'm *finally* ready, and I don't want to wait for even a second longer.

Traffic is horrid, in and of itself, without my added irritation. I'm so glad I don't have to drive in rush hour every day. How can people stand it? I feel like such an awful person. When I passed the accident this morning, I briefly wished to see my husband's Jag crumpled amongst the debris. Wouldn't life be so much easier if he were dead, though?

I'm really glad that Claire and I have weekend plans. Since she walked out, I've been having serious Claire withdrawals. The days have been unbelievably long without her. I'm not used to being alone on the job. I have no one to hang out with anymore. No one to eat lunch with. No one to share work duties with. Honestly, I think I get a lot more work done now that she's gone. Claire was my beautiful distraction.

Oh well. After today, I only have five more work days until I say "adios" to this shithole forever. I just found out this morning that I got the job at Binded! I am so psyched to start working there. Ray said the reason he wanted to interview me was so he could get a feel for what I was looking for in the position. He suggested doing the art show thing every single weekend, and I can use it toward my regular hours. Sandra told him I got rejected by a "real" gallery, and he jumped at the chance to have a steady art crowd flowing through. I will get paid to stand around and yap with people about my paintings. I'm in heaven just picturing it. No pun intended. Ha!

God, I love that woman. She is the one who gave me the confidence to try to paint in the first place. How did she even see that in me immediately after meeting? Look at us now. If someone would've told me a few months ago that this was the path I would be on today, I would've laughed my ass off at them. There's no chance I would've believed if someone said I would have a steady art gig this soon. Everything is going to be so much better after I switch jobs. I hope it's better for Sandra, too. At least this way, I can kind of watch over her.

Some people believe there is a silver lining in every dark cloud. Never had I truly appreciated that until I was informed of Tiffany's newfound employment. Since Ray plans to have the gallery every weekend, she will be working part-time hours with me during the week and still receive full-time benefits for being in the gallery on the weekends. I'm so thrilled for her! Things are really starting to fall into place. I cannot describe the joy and pride that I feel for what she has accomplished in such a short amount of time.

I mailed off a final draft of my poem. How exhilarating to chase this dream! Entering a contest, even though my talent has collected dust for years, has given me a new sense of what I'm looking to accomplish in life. I just want experiences. If I don't end up benefitting financially from my writing, I still feel renewed from only the process. Pursuing a goal, no matter how small – like walking one little envelope to the mail – has its rewards. I won't let myself be too excited about the contest because the odds of winning are slim to none. I'm just relieved I entered at all. I feel so alive! Alive as never before.

So far, this weekend is better than I ever expected. Claire took CeeCee over to her mom's, so we're officially child-free until Sunday morning. She is the cutest baby in America, but Claire needs a break. She is so upset with herself for getting emotional and walking out of work. She is trying to blow off the guilt by continually reminding herself what it was like to work for Bob. Carl wasn't even mad because he can handle their finances. He has heard so many stories and complaints, he didn't like her working there anyway. Sandra gave me the name of her lawyer to give to Claire, but I doubt she has a solid case. Obviously, I'm unable to consult Tee any longer. Duh. I can't consult with that dick about anything. What a weirdo he ended up being.

Sandra said she has this private lawyer that she goes to without her husband's knowledge. She met her at a Christmas party right before she found out Anthony was a wifebeater (which she admitted has been going on for way longer than she told me at first.) She contacted her a short time after the first incident and was almost persuaded to press charges against him. She never did follow through, but she and the attorney remained in contact all these years. Sandra said she was planning on seeing her sometime next week about a living will and would give her a heads up about Claire's work grievance. Once again, my friend is going out of her way to help someone else.

This weekend is dragging by, and I can feel myself deteriorating bit by bit. My husband is out doing Lord-knows-what, and I'm left alone to ponder my existence. After unsuccessfully trying to contact Liam, I reluctantly sat down to journal. Sitting uneasily in my chair, with shutters drawn and lights all ablaze, I think again about my potential stalker. I am *positive* that someone has been following me. I don't even know how I would know or why I so concretely believe I'm sure. I just *sense* that someone is near. There is no logical explanation, nor a single fact to back up my fears. I just know I am so frightened that my hand shakes as I write these very words. I'm gripping my pepper spray keychain in my left hand, but would it even help me in a time of need? I strongly believe in intuition and, without the presence of a crowded bookstore, I realize that I am definitely feeling observed and vulnerable. I was raised to follow my instincts.

"With a gut feeling," my mother began, "you're given an answer and a choice. If you go with your instinct, you may be rewarded for your subconscious observations. If you habitually ignore your intuition, you'll be mentally plagued for the rest of your days, constantly questioning your decisions." Are you completely satisfied with your current situation? Should you ignore it? No, I want a more rewarding life. I cannot ignore my gut on this one. Instincts should be finely tuned as you evolve. You should be able to gauge how reliable your natural gifts are. Animal instincts are often lost to us humans. We are so self-absorbed, heads constantly tucked away in our phones, ignoring everything (and sometimes everyone) around us.

Watch, listen intently and purposefully and pay close attention to that little whisper in the back of your mind. That voice is literally *always* right. Someday, you may know that an enemy is near just by realizing you have goosebumps – or *truth bumps*, as I've heard them called. Did a wild thought cross your mind and later came true right before your eyes? Déjà vu? Listen to it. *Heed your fear*, everything around me is screaming. When I am not wallowing in fear, I have no choice but to sit and wait. The danger is coming, as sure as the season's change, I am certain of it.

It has been a really nice weekend so far, and Claire wants to wash her car. She just bought a vintage Monte Carlo SS a couple of months ago, and she's still in the obsessive phase of her ownership. Keeping it perfectly spotless is a complete understatement for how immaculate that car is. I don't know how she does it with a kid and a man around! Since she was going to be outside for a while, I decided to call Tom's cell and see if he misses me. He does! Apparently, his sister went into labor this morning, and did I even know she was pregnant? I don't remember him mentioning it, but I guess that's normal for a guy. Anyway, he's on his way to the hospital preparing to be an uncle. Super exciting! I bet he'll be so great with kids. Maybe a bit of a bad influence with his rotten sense of humor, though. As I was gabbing his ear off about how happy I am to be leaving A & A, I glanced out the window and saw someone talking to Claire outside next to her car. He's really nice looking. Is it a neighbor? A friend?

I joked to Tom, "Ohhhh, Carl may have some older competition down the block! Wait. That's weird. Let me call you back in a little bit, hon." Obviously, he's not a neighbor. He just got into his car and left, and it was parked on the street instead of in a driveway. Claire turned off the hose and left her precious car full of suds. She dropped the nozzle, turned toward the house, and took off running for the front door. *Is she crying?*

I am so sick of isolating myself inside this dreadful house. Whether I am in here or out there, if someone is going to attack me, what does it even matter? What will even happen that I haven't already experienced inside these walls? If they want to get me, they'd best be prepared for a fight. I have decided to go out and take in some gardening and some good old fashioned vitamin D therapy. It is such an amazing pastime and those endorphins should vastly improve my bleak mood. I am already a prisoner in my own head. It's time I break free of this house that keeps me nervously bound inside, even if I only venture out to the yard.

Put me out of my misery. End this dreadful karmic punishment of mine. Let's get it over with already. I proposition the air, willing disaster to befall me. How fickle am I, teetering from terror to dauntlessness on a whim? I'm greeted by only afternoon sunshine, cheerfully chirping birds and the promise of a total body workout. You get what you give, so I'll give my garden all of this pent up energy I'm feeling. Everything evens out in the end, they say. I was raised in a way to be pleasant to everyone that crosses my path even if they slither up to me like a sneaky little predator. A perfect combination of etiquette and positive karmic energy. A codependent cycle, based on the presumption that if I always walk the straight path, life will reward me in return. A false presumption, thus far. A venomous snake could be ready to strike, poison sitting in wait on the edge of his fangs, aiming straight for my jugular, and I'll be damned if I'd not smile to greet him. Pumping the air with my hand outstretched like an idiot. *I am a joke.*

"Nice to 'meat' you, Mr. Snake, can I get you anything before you begin? A tasty vein or artery for starters. Our special today is a bored housewife with a good aura and broken karma over a lovely bed of hostile dementia. Very sweet, no samples. Pay in full, I assure you this one is devoted to the end. *S-S-She'll never fight back, you'll s-s-s-seeee.*" I welcome death to a great extent. Blessed I'd be to serve my purpose elsewhere, to see what secrets other worlds may hold. Unless my broken karma can follow me to the afterlife as well? *I am us-s-sed to it; I welcome it s-s-soooo, for leaving here will be s-s-such s-s-solace.*

Claire is scared shitless, and I am frightened for her. She is so freaked out that she hardly remembers anything from her conversation with the man outside. She doesn't even know his name or what part of town he said he was from. I fired questions at her, barely any of which she could answer.

"GEEZ, CLAIRE!" I screamed at her. She said she saw his credentials, and he told her to go inside "immediately" because he thought she could be in danger.

"I believe someone is stalking you or this property for some reason," he advised. "Who else lives here, ma'am? I am filing a police report on your behalf, so they may contact you for further questioning." That was, roughly, what he said. Claire is so mental over this. We're both really happy Ciera is at her grandma's house tonight. Was this person waiting for Carl to leave or what? I don't get it. We need more info! Whoever is stalking her isn't out there right now, the guy assured her. It doesn't matter, though. We're not taking any chances tonight, so we're heading over to Tom's. Hopefully, he'll be back from the hospital by the time we get over there. After talking Claire down from her state of absolute hysteria, Carl decided to cut his fishing trip short to come home. The only problem is he won't be back for another eight hours. Claire needs to hurry the fuck up and gather her shit. I am not trying to stay here any longer than we have to. I'm feeling super uncomfortable and want to get to Tom's as soon as possible.

The inner turmoil of everything in my life is becoming too much to bear. I can no longer sit and wait for my destiny – my undeniable fate. I feel I must take control now before I lose my courage. I have placed all of the evidence against Anthony in the trunk of my car. Along with this, I included the bare necessities of living. All I really need is a toothbrush, a hairbrush, and a couple of outfits. I have a trust, so I don't need Anthony for stability. I don't want very many reminders of this life anyhow. Best to just start over. When I look in the mirror, I no longer want to see a woman who lives a shameful existence. I want to see a brand-new being in her place. Perhaps a working woman with a smart business suit. Someone independent and constantly striving to earn her keep and prove she is worthy. Someone that leaves her own unique mark on society. That's the person I want to see staring back at me. Not a meek woman on the verge of a mental breakdown. When I took the photographs of my beaten face, I thought I needed to use them against my husband. Their purpose has already been fulfilled, I finally realized. They forced me to face my truth.

I am almost ready to leave; I am almost ready to *live.* I only need to write my farewell letter and then walk out that door one last time. I know I can find my strength tomorrow when the light of day is upon me once again. If only Liam would return my call. I'm so scared to pursue this freedom while not having his watchful eyes upon me. I know it's never going to happen, but I'd not hesitate to run straight into his arms. I wonder what it would be like to feel his embrace. Would my freedom change how we relate? I'll never know. It makes it so much more difficult to run away when there is nothing to run to.

I feel like a scared little hermit crab trapped inside my shell. I can only imagine what Claire must be feeling right now. We are over at Tom's alone and won't even open the door to get the fucking newspaper. Since when did it become such a life-altering decision that it takes ten minutes to figure out if we need the Everyday section bad enough? Turns out, we don't need it that bad. Since we found out about Claire's stalker, we cannot stop talking about the weirdness of this situation. This absolutely, positively sucks. I wish one of the guys would get here because we're feeling underprepared to physically defending ourselves against a crazy person. Where did our overconfident kick-ass attitude go? I can't stand feeling powerless.

CHAPTER 19

Yesterday, I felt a lot better after working in the garden, but today I feel like I am losing it again. What happened? I had such resolve, such conviction that I am ready. Have I conjured up an imaginary danger in my head in order to self-sabotage my plan? I want to say that I'm certain about a stalker, but the more I think about my unsteady mental health, the more I question if it's real.

I keep feeling like every time I turn around, someone is stepping just outside of my view. I am carrying my pepper spray around at all times now, and at what a bargain -- $17 seems like a steal. I have had a death grip on it for days now. It says it should be replaced every three years, but I would assume it would maintain some potency after that time period. Is it like when ibuprofen expires? Just use a little more? I mean, I would drain this entire canister in one attack, so that was never in question. I plan to hold that button down until there is either no spray or no criminal. Whether it is three days or three years, I will use an appropriate amount to render my assailant good for nothing. I refuse to take chances and, honestly, I'd very much appreciate witnessing a perp's eyes swelling up. Then I could pull off his ears just like we learned in class. Three pounds of pressure, remember? Because of the spray, he won't be able to see where I throw his ears after I pull them off. *Poor thing.*

I feel like a brand new person today! Tom came home last night and after we ate dinner with Claire, we all watched a movie. A comedy, of course. We needed it. Carl got there to pick up Claire, and they decided to stay at her mom's for the rest of the night. Tom thought I should stay home from work and skip self-defense class, but I wouldn't hear of it. First of all, I'm on my last few days of working at A & A. I need to give them the respect of working my full two weeks. Not! I'm so full of shit. The gossip around the office has been juicy as fuck since Claire bounced. It's literally the only reason I've stuck around.

Who would even be following me?. My husband? A hitman? My family? All I ever wanted was happiness, and I have never had the luxury of that. Why would someone want to cause me even more misery? I wasn't always this way, a nervous wreck. I was a cheerful, kind child. Through the years, I've found brief periods of joy. When Liam was present, I always felt content. He felt like home. Worries are forgotten and libido awakened, How can I convince him to see me again? First things first: It is time I leave my husband to ensure I've even the slightest chance at happiness.

I'm so stoked I came to work today. What showed up? A dozen red roses with the whitest baby's breath I have ever seen, that's what. Every bitch up in that office had their jealous eyes on me as I pulled out the card.

I enjoyed seeing you last night. I can't wait to see you again.

Tom is playing a game I could get used to. I swear he is the most undercover romantic I have ever gone out with. I tried to call to thank him, but it went straight to voicemail. He's probably at the hospital visiting the new baby. Cells barely have service at that hospital. I love that he is my "secret admirer" and didn't sign the card. I've never had surprise roses before. Fun shit! With a signed card or not, the secret is out: Tom is totally falling for me!

I have wasted my whole damn life. The duration of my entire adulthood has been spent drowning in self-pity and envious feelings for the happy couples around me. It stops now. I will no longer sit and feel sorry for the path that I, myself, have chosen. Now, I will be free to choose another option. Plan B. Hopefully, a better existence is on the horizon. *God, give me strength. Please, let me know I am ready for this.*

I swung by Tom's after work to thank him in person, and there were more roses outside his door. Like, a lot more. How did he even know I would show up? They would've ended up a wilted mess if I had gone straight home after the office.

Every envelope had a number on the outside, and the lowest was Number 2. I assume Number 1 was delivered while I was at work, so I started there and went in order:

2. I enjoy seeing you every day.

Awwww, he is too sweet.

3. I enjoy seeing you every night.

Mmmhmm. Well, we both know why you enjoy that, you dirty boy!

4. I enjoyed seeing you in the shower this morning.

Wait. Tom wasn't even home this morning. Was he?

5. I'll take care of my wife.

Ummm... marriage? Slow your roll.

6. And clean my knife for you.

So the police just left. When I finally got ahold of Tom, I freaked out on him BIG TIME for not answering his cell earlier. Not that it's really his fault, but had I known he didn't send the first bouquet, maybe I wouldn't have been here all alone to find these weird and scary messages. At least, I would've known right when I pulled up that something wasn't right. If I knew the first bouquet was from a mystery sender, I would've immediately called the cops or left. Tom is on his way home from visiting his fam at the hospital now, and I don't know that I've ever been so scared in all my life.

WHAT IN THE ACTUAL FUCK IS GOING ON?

I told the police that some guy told Claire that she had a stalker, and they said this crazy psycho killer (I may be paraphrasing here) probably was watching ME over at her place. That never even cross my mind at the time, but duh! We wondered why someone was messing with her out of the blue. Claire and Carl have been together for a long time, and she never entertains other dick options, so we were clueless about who would even be stalking her.

I mentioned to the police that Tee had been a regular at Tom's bar and that he had recently threatened him. He definitely could've followed one of us home at any time. It doesn't make sense, though. We never even had sex. I can't figure this maniac out and why he's so crazy over me. The relationship never even went anywhere. I didn't even know his full name or where he lived, honestly. What's his angle? And does he really have a wife? I feel like a terrible person. This makes me sick to my stomach. I can't believe I was messing with a married man, and I'm so glad I never slept with him. I mean, I hope I would've asked his last name first, now that I think about it. The police are going to Caesar's to question a few other employees to see if they have any additional information to add or witnessed anything strange lately.

Where is Tom? The locksmith is here to change the locks, and I just don't understand why he's not home yet. Probably stuck in traffic since it's almost rush hour, but geez! I still need to call Claire and let her know that the freak she was warned about is most likely a freak for *me*. She should still be careful, though. I'm not going to tell Sandra. She has nothing to do with this, and she shouldn't have to deal with my drama on top of her own. That poor woman has enough stress. Also, she never liked Tee in the first place. How could I be so damn wrong about him? I'm so embarrassed.

Dear Anthony,

I am having trouble recalling the exact moment where it all went wrong. I concretely know that I cannot take this life anymore. The strain that our dysfunctional marriage has put on my physical and mental health tips the scales, and its extent may never really be known because I have never truly been left to grow into my own person. I have been so unhappy for such a long time. I entered into this relationship believing marriage was sacred but now I'm just scared. I am scared of my own husband – the one person in my life that I have chosen as a purposeful partner. I always wonder which of your masks you'll don before walking through our door: will I be with the handsome, charismatic man that proposed or the demonic monster you've managed to become? At times, I wond

I just called Claire. She was standing in Sandra's lawyer's office discussing whether or not she has a case to bring against Bob and A & A. She said she would call me back in a few minutes which is fine because Tom is finally home. We need to sit down for dinner, but I'm still so freaked out. I can't get ahold of Sandra, and we're supposed to go to class tonight. I don't think we should even go now. What if someone follows us there, and I end up leading a crazy person to a roomful of women? I wasn't going to tell her about my stalker stuff, but then I remembered how she babbled on and on about being watched, and I feel like I need to let her know now. After all, Claire and Tom were both compromised because of my mess, and who knows how Sandra's husband would react if he noticed some random guy hanging around her place. Her voicemail isn't picking up. It just rings and rings and rings. It's so strange. I'm getting a really awful feeling. I think I'm going to throw up.

Claire just called me back and was completely frantic. Sandra's old private investigator friend called the lawyer's office while she was standing right there. Sandra's in the hospital, she's unconscious, and there are no additional details. I need to go up there right now! *What is happening?*

We're at Mercy General, and one of my closest friends is on life support. The staff told me that Liam Hanson is being examined right now and after he is through talking with the police, I can meet with him. I finally get to see the man that had Sandra's face lighting up. I'm so sad that it's under these circumstances. *Oh my God.* I just remembered that Sandra made it very clear she wanted the plug pulled if she was ever on life support. I'm going to lose her. I can't handle this. Tom was just at this very hospital welcoming a new life into this world. Just a few floors away, families are shedding tears of joy and praising God for these precious new lives. They've so much promise for the future; already the apple of their parents' eyes.

And here we are, standing around waiting to let someone die that is so special to me. A person that is so *deserving* of a life after this. I can't believe I'll never see her again. It's not fair. I'm not ready to lose her. They let me go in to see her, and she looks pretty bad. Really bad, actually. Severely beat up and swollen literally everywhere. The machines are so eerie. There are so many wires and sounds buzzing and beeping around her. They said she was stabbed repeatedly in the abdomen and thrown down a flight of stairs.

Her family is on their way. At least they'll be here with her when she goes.

I met Liam right before I went in to see her. I understand what she sees in him. Wow, he is really good looking! He asked to speak with me privately after my visit with Sandra. "It's very urgent," he advised before I walked away to see my friend.

After I left her room, I walked up to Liam and asked, "Do you know what happened?" It hit me like a ton of bricks: *this is the man that was talking to Claire outside her house. What in the world?*

He whispered quietly, "Tiffany, Tee is Anthony."

"I'm sorry? Anthony who? I don't know any Anthony."

"You were dating Sandra's husband."

I stumbled backward a little, my whole body covered in goosebumps. Liam stabled me and I sat down, in shock, as he told me everything. "Tee" had been romancing several young women, including his secretary at his law firm, which is the woman in the photos he'd provided to Sandra. *No wonder she said she didn't trust lawyers.* When he realized that Anthony was stalking someone a few weeks ago, he decided to keep trailing him. He followed him to A & A Chemicals while I was at work, but when the trail led him to Claire's, he assumed she was the one he was after. Rightly so, too, because while she was outside washing her car, Liam inquired if she worked at the chemical company, and she confirmed she had.

Sandra felt like she was being followed because she was. By Liam. He cut ties with her because, yes, it's inappropriate to maintain any kind of relationship under the circumstances they were in. In reality, he wanted to keep her safe. That meant no distractions, no mistakes, and no "gallivanting" around – as Sandra would say. My eyes welled up with tears for my friend. She didn't even know how much he really cared for her, and now she will never have the chance to. Liam knew from trailing Tee – I mean, Anthony – that he was going off the deep end and about to blow. And he did. After ordering the creepy flowers for me, he headed home, where he found Sandra preparing her farewell letter.

She was finally leaving him. Oh, God, it feels so ironic. Life is tragic.

Liam said she put up a damn good fight before she fell unconscious at the base of the staircase. He didn't come through the door until it was too late. As Anthony ran down the stairs, presumably to finish her off, Liam shot him twice. The first shot was fatal. Anthony is dead. Tee is dead. And Sandra will shortly follow.

I walked away feeling very drained. I went back to sit next to my friend. I was holding her hand and talking quietly to her when the news came through. *Her living will was never notarized, so it's deemed invalid.* I don't know if it even matters, but at least there is a small chance she could live. These machines hold my friend's fate now. It feels even more unfair now. We get to keep her but under what terms? Like this? And for how long?

I'm going to lose it. My chest heaves as I sob next to her bed, soaking my face. Liam drops a heavy stack of notebooks on the bedside table next to me and asks me to read them. They're her journals. Packed with details and dreams, they weave such tales. I had no idea she wanted to become a published author. She has such passion and her writing is so eloquent. I'm determined to help her.

Sandra has been on life support for three weeks. Legally, it cannot be removed, as no one close to her will sign for that. It's kinda funny, really. I read in her journal that the notary was coming back from vacation on, what turned out to be, the day after her accident. Had this happened one day later, she wouldn't be with us still.

I talk to her often. The day has finally come for all her dreams to come true. I tell her of all the good news waiting for her out here. Her husband is no longer a threat. Liam is every bit of the scrumptious morsel she dreamt he was. He does love her and admits he felt an undeniable connection from the very first moment their eyes met.

And she won second place in the poetry contest she entered. Amazing! I am so proud of my friend even as my heart aches.

I've been spending so much time at her bedside, just willing her to awaken and reclaim what's waiting for her. I met her mother, who is such a lovely woman, and her sister, Sue. Her *identical twin* sister. There are some things in life that people should mention out of courtesy, don't you think? I don't even want to know what my face looked like when I saw someone identical to Sandra walking toward me.

They are really supportive of what I'm doing for her. Excited even. They assured me I'm making her dream come true by compiling our journals to form a novel. The whole story is told between her journal and mine. Where

I leave something out, she fills in the gaps and vice versa. I'm going to make sure her name is in print. I will publish our story and, together, we will prove how small the world really is. *Just like Sandra had told me.* That there is no such thing a coincidence.

She's awake.

EPILOGUE

When I woke from a vegetative state after a month's time, I was showered with love and affection, to say the least. Liam was at my side, and my worried mother looked upon us. My story (the condensed version, at least) was on the ten o'clock news, and my family was by my side for the broadcast. *My family.* It's really a dream come true. They said Tiffany consistently willed me to fight. Every single day, she talked about how brave and strong I was and that it was okay for me to come back.

"Because he is gone forever, and you are safe."

I wouldn't have blamed any of my friends or family if they'd lost hope and decided to let me go. But everything happens for a reason, I truly believe this sentiment. My broken karma has long since found its repair. My life was almost taken by my own husband's hand, a reality that is much more common than people realize. I've been able to make a full recovery and, although it's been a long road both mentally and physically, I refuse to let the ugly moments of my past dictate my future.

I remarried, and I couldn't wait to take my new husband's name. It's Sandra Hanson now, thank you very much. I have waited so long for this amount of joy, and I know I will never take any of it for granted. For several years now, our house has been filled with boisterous laughter, countless friends, and the best family anyone could ask for. Tiffany is my most treasured friend aside from my sister. Liam and Tom get along very well, so we try to spend one evening a week either out and about or just staying in to play games or watch a movie. Life has never felt so *normal.* It's sensational. The feeling of togetherness is so strong – so concrete – that it's difficult to even imagine that I was unhappy for so many years. Admittedly, our household doesn't *sound* very happy at the moment. It's full of tears, actually. In all my life, I never knew a cry could sound so sweet.

"Is someone hungry?" I smile down at our princess, constantly amazed and continuously grateful for moments like this. We named her Eden. It means "place of pleasure."

THE END*

This doesn't have to be the end.

You are not alone, and you are loved.

HELP IS AVAILABLE 24/7. IF YOU ARE IN AN

EMERGENCY SITUATION, PLEASE CALL 911.

National Suicide Prevention Lifeline

1-800-273-8255 or TTY dial 771 first or

en Español 1-888-628-9454

www.suicidepreventionlifeline.org

National Domestic Violence Hotline

1-800-799-7233 or TTY 1-800-787-3224 or

text LOVEIS to1-866-331-9474

www.thehotline.org

National Sexual Assault Hotline

1-800-656-HOPE (4673)

Made in the USA
Columbia, SC
29 July 2021

42520788R00107